KATE AND THE KRAKEN

A SCIFI ALIEN ROMANCE
(ALIEN ABDUCTION BOOK 11)

HONEY PHILLIPS

Copyright © 2021 by Honey Phillips

All rights reserved. No part of this book may be used or reproduced by any means, graphic, electronic, or mechanical, including photocopying, recording, taping or by any information storage retrieval system without the written permission of the author.

Disclaimer

This book is a work of fiction. Names, characters, places, and incidents are products of the author's imagination or are used fictitiously and are not to be construed as real. Any resemblance to actual events, locales, organizations, or people, living or dead, is entirely coincidental.

Cover by Maria Spada Book Cover Design
Edited by Lindsay York at LY Publishing Services

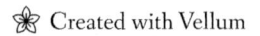

Created with Vellum

CHAPTER ONE

The escape pod smashed into the ocean with a shock that reverberated through Kate's body, despite the restraints holding her in place. Through the small porthole, she could see a cloud of steam and a giant plume of water, rapidly replaced by bubbles jetting up through a deep jade-colored sea as the pod plunged down into the water. Oh, God, no. The thought of being entombed at the bottom of an alien ocean terrified her. But then the direction of the bubbles changed and a little later, the pod popped back up on the surface.

The aqua-colored sky swung past in dizzying circles until the pod finally settled into the same rhythm as the surrounding waves. Her stomach rolled just as erratically before finally calming enough that she could take stock of her situation.

The padding behind her was thin and worn, but although her back felt bruised and sore, she hadn't suffered any major injuries. The restraints across her head, waist, thighs, and ankles had prevented her from being flung around the small space and undoubtedly breaking her neck. Not that she had appreciated them when they had been strapped around her.

Eshak, one of the aliens who had abducted her, had shoved her into the pod without any explanation. When she'd tried to demand an answer, he simply leered at her and grabbed her breasts, squeezing them painfully. Her arms were unrestrained and she responded instinctively, slapping his face.

He growled and raised his own hand, but before he could return the blow, Yakshi appeared. Another one of the guards, he was usually less brutal than Eshak.

"What the hell are you doing? We need to get these females off the ship before that Royal Fleet ship catches up with us."

Eshak scowled. "I still think the captain is panicking. We don't know that they're coming after us."

"Do you want to take the chance and spend the rest of your life on one of the Emperor's prison planets? Now get moving."

"But she slapped me." Eshak's scowl turned lecherous. "That means I get to punish her."

"It will have to wait until we pick them up. Now go."

Yakshi shoved Eshak, and he grumbled but moved away. Was he going after one of her friends now? Before she could ask, Yakshi slammed the door to the pod closed with a loud clang. The capsule lurched, then the acceleration forced her back against the thin padding as it launched itself into space.

As the pod plummeted towards a strange planet, she'd caught a brief glimpse of wide green seas and small scattered islands, but she had been distracted by the increasing heat in the small space. Although the temperature became painfully hot, the shielding had prevented the pod from burning up as it entered the atmosphere, and the air cooled rapidly once the pod hit the water.

Now that her heaving stomach had settled, she could evaluate the situation logically. Although being abandoned on a strange planet wouldn't have been her first choice, maybe it represented a chance to finally escape from her captors. There had been little she could do while caged on an alien spaceship, but now that she was on land—or at least the surface of the planet—there should be more possibilities.

Aliens. She still couldn't believe she had been kidnapped by aliens. She had been working late in her lab, as usual, when she realized that she had missed the daily walk that was her minimal concession to the need for exercise. The beautifully landscaped grounds surrounding the lab complex offered a number of walking trails, and she had followed her favorite one around the small lake, knowing that she would be back at her desk in thirteen minutes.

Although it was close to midnight, the trail was well lit and she had never considered the possibility of danger in the gated grounds. But as she took the picturesque bridge over the artificial waterfall, she caught a whiff of something unpleasant, followed by a stinging pain in her neck. She'd had just enough time to wonder why on earth somebody would want to drug her before darkness took her.

The next thing she knew, she woke up in a cage. A small, plump blonde smiled at her sympathetically from an adjoining cage.

"Does your head hurt? I had a terrible headache when I woke up, but it didn't last very long. You'll be fine in a few minutes."

The other woman gave her a sunny smile as Kate stared at her in disbelief.

"Fine? You've got to be kidding. Where are we?"

The woman's smile faltered. "I know this is going to sound crazy, but we've been kidnapped by aliens."

"Aliens? Don't be ridiculous," Kate snapped. The woman in the other cage was wearing a much too brief white outfit that barely covered her generous curves, and her curly blonde hair was in pigtails, of all things. How could Kate take her seriously?

But then she realized that her own practical khakis and button-down shirt had been replaced with an identical outfit—a white shift dress that only fastened at her shoulders and her waist. Since she was nowhere near as well-endowed, it covered more, but it was still far more revealing than anything she had ever worn before.

Her fingers clenched in the silky fabric as she looked around. Cages lined both sides of a curved corridor, filled with an astonishing array of animals—animals that could not have come from Earth. Zoology had never been one of her main interests, but she was quite sure no Earth animal had three legs like the pink-furred one in the cage directly across from her.

"Aliens?" she asked the other woman again, but this time it really wasn't a question.

"Mmhmm." The woman nodded emphatically, her pigtails bouncing. "Can you believe it? I always thought that UFOs existed, but I never thought one would come and get me! I'm Mary, by the way."

"I'm Dr. Kate Richards," she said automatically, then winced. "I mean, call me Kate. Have you been here long?"

"I'm not really sure." Mary's face wrinkled into a cute little frown. "A guard came by and gave me some food a couple of times."

Mary gestured to the front of her cage where two bowls were attached to the bars, one filled with water and the other with a greenish-colored mush. The sight horrified Kate. It wasn't so much the food—she was so frequently distracted by work that she lived on cereal and fast food—but the clear indication that whoever had taken them regarded them as little more than animals. Her own work didn't involve upper-level organisms, but she had seen enough of her colleagues' labs that the resemblance to the housing of lab animals was indisputable.

Was this some kind of experiment? And who was doing the experimenting?

"Are the guards aliens?" she asked.

"I think they have to be, don't you? Although they do look kind of human, not green or anything. They're not too bad." A shadow crossed Mary's face. "Not most of them, anyway."

"Did they tell you anything? Can you even understand them?"

The pigtails bounced again as Mary nodded. "They put something in our ears. I saw them do it to you when they put you in the cage."

Kate immediately probed her ear, recoiling when she felt something warm in her ear canal that pulsed slightly at her touch. It felt biological, but if it truly acted as a translator, there must have been more involved. Perhaps biomechanical? Her mind started to follow that trail, but then Mary suddenly stiffened. Her smile looked a little more forced as she glanced over at Kate.

"That's the not-so-nice one. It's better just to keep quiet."

Kate followed her gaze to the approaching male. Dressed in a sloppy black uniform, he definitely could have passed as human, albeit an unusually short, hairy one. His heavily ridged brow reminded her of the pictures of Neanderthal man in her anthropology textbook. *Perhaps there's some common ancestry,* she thought, fascinated despite her horror. The guard came to a halt in front of her cage.

"You don't look like you'll fetch many credits at auction," he sneered, running his eyes over her. As Mary had said, Kate could understand him perfectly.

"Then perhaps you shouldn't have taken me," she said tartly. "Why don't you take me—us—back?"

He laughed, revealing sharp yellow teeth. "Not much is better than nothing. I wouldn't have picked you myself. But if you can convince me you're worth it, I can make your life a lot more pleasant." He grabbed his crotch, his meaning all too clear, and she recoiled in disgust. She had always found the thought of intimate relations with another human vaguely disgusting, and she certainly had no desire to change her mind with this primitive specimen.

He scowled at her obvious horror and leaned close to the bars. An offensive odor, the same one she had detected just before she was taken, washed over her.

"Then you'd better keep your mouth shut. Otherwise, I get to punish you. And then you'll be too busy screaming to talk," he snarled and walked away.

To Kate's surprise, her hands were actually shaking. She'd been insulted many times before, but no one had ever so overtly threatened her with violence. When she looked over at Mary, her face was pale, but she managed to smile.

"See what I mean? Not very nice. But they're not all like that."

Kate turned her head away before she snapped at Mary's unfounded optimism. Didn't the other woman realize that their situation was only going to get worse? Auctioned off by alien slavers? She shuddered as her imagination conjured up their probable fate. She had always relied on research and intelligence to make her way through life, but for the first time, she didn't think they would help. She buried her face in her knees and gave in to despair.

CHAPTER TWO

Despite Kate's apprehension, Mary turned out to be right. Another guard appeared sometime later, but all he did was fill up their food and water bowls, barely glancing at them before moving along the line of cages and repeating the process. Almost all of the occupants were given the same food, although a few of the animals received something that looked more like raw meat. Given their rather impressive teeth, she suspected they were pure carnivores. Mush was definitely a better option.

The next guard who showed up seemed to be doing an inspection, checking the occupants of the cages against a tablet. Like the first two, he wore a plain black uniform, but he had what looked like an insignia on his shoulder and she decided he must be in charge. He paused outside Mary's cage.

"You were provided with sufficient nutrition?" he asked.

"Oh, yes, thank you, Yakshi." Mary smiled at him. "I'm just not very hungry."

"You need to eat." He hesitated, glancing around, then pulled a foil wrapped package out of his pocket and dropped it into her bowl. "You may find this more palatable."

"Are you sure? I don't want you to get into any trouble."

Kate did her best to hide her disbelief. Mary actually looked concerned about the guard.

"No one will challenge me," Yakshi assured her.

"Where are you taking us?" Kate asked, determined to get some answers.

His brows immediately drew together into a frightening scowl. "That is not your concern, human."

"If it's money you're after, I have access to a large bank account," she persisted, undeterred by his thunderous expression. "I can convert it into gold or jewels."

"There is nothing on your planet I want." For the briefest second, his eyes flicked back to Mary. "Now be silent, or I will be forced to punish you."

Unlike the previous guard, he didn't seem excited by the prospect, but she had no doubt that he would carry through on the threat.

"She's just new, Yakshi," Mary said soothingly. "I promise she'll be good."

Yakshi looked down at her, his face softening slightly, then dipped his head. "See that she is."

He strode off down the corridor without another word.

"He's the nice one?" Kate asked in disbelief.

"He's really not that bad. I just think he's under a lot of stress. And look." Mary tore open a foil wrapped package to reveal something that looked rather like a protein bar. The color was an unappetizing grey, but it smelled like chocolate. Mary broke it in half and offered her the largest piece.

"Are you sure you want to share this?" Kate asked.

"Of course. Somehow, I don't think you're going to win him over."

Mary's blue eyes twinkled at her, and Kate raised her eyebrows.

"Did you put on that sweet, helpless little act on purpose?"

"I really wasn't very hungry, but my mama always said you catch more flies with honey than vinegar."

Kate smiled in spite of herself. "I'm afraid vinegar is more my style."

"So? I make a wonderful vinegar pie. You can always transform ingredients."

"I'll take your word for that."

As they munched their protein bar—which wasn't exactly chocolate, but tasty enough—Mary told her more about herself. She was a kindergarten teacher and a recent newcomer to the Gulf Coast. The aliens had captured her on the beach not far from Kate's lab.

"I should have known better than to try jogging," Mary said with a rueful smile, looking down at her generous curves.

"Jogging?" Kate asked doubtfully. She had never seen the appeal.

"My doctor said I needed more exercise. I like to watch the sun come up over the water so I figured I could kill two birds with one stone and run at sunrise." She wrinkled her nose. "I can't say I was enjoying it, but then something bit my neck and I passed out. I woke up here."

Tears sparkled in Mary's big blue eyes, but she gave Kate a tremulous smile. "I'm sorry you were taken, but I'm glad I'm not alone anymore."

"I understand." She'd always been a loner, but having a companion was surprisingly comforting.

"Did you grow up in the area?" Mary asked.

"No, but I've been here—there—since I was an undergraduate. After I got my doctorate, I went to work for an organization studying carbon recycling in the ocean. We get most of our samples off the coast."

"You didn't want to teach?"

"God, no." She shuddered. "I was a teaching assistant while getting my doctorate and that was bad enough. I didn't like teaching, and my students didn't like me."

"I'm sure that's not true," Mary protested. "I can already tell how smart you are."

"That's not always an advantage," Kate said dryly. "I bet your students love you."

Mary's smile faltered, and Kate realized how she must have sounded. "Oh, crap, I'm sorry. I didn't mean it like that. But now you can see why I wasn't good at teaching. Or anything that requires interaction with other people, actually."

"I'll just have to teach you to use a little more honey. It will make your life easier, wherever we end up."

They sat in silence for a few minutes, and then Kate sighed. "Can you hand me that foil please?"

"I'm afraid there isn't anything left," Mary said as she handed it over.

"That's not why I wanted it." She leaned forward to examine the lock on the cage. "This appears to be an electronic lock. I might be able to use the foil to disrupt the signal and open the cage."

"Really?" Mary's eyes widened, but then she bit her lip. "And then what?"

Hmm. She had been focused on the immediate problem, but Mary was right. What were the next logical steps?

"Find the transporter room, I think."

"Transporter room? Like in Star Trek?"

"Or something equivalent. It's hard to believe that they're flying in and out of our atmosphere without being detected."

"You think we could just beam back home?"

"I don't know," she admitted. "But I think we're still close."

"Why?"

Kate gestured at the empty cage next to hers. "I'm afraid they're looking for someone else."

As if in answer to her words, a guard appeared. A stretcher floated behind him, another woman dressed in white strapped to the surface. He paused outside the empty cage, and Kate watched as he pressed a small black oval into the woman's ear canal, then unfastened the straps and dumped her body on the floor of the cage.

He looked down at her, then over to Kate and Mary, and grinned. It was not a pleasant expression.

"Not a bad haul. The three of you are going to make us a nice little profit."

"You can't do this," Kate said urgently. "We're people. We have lives. You can't just sell us."

"Why not?" He shrugged. "There's quite an underground market for human slaves. Apparently, you're very fuckable."

"Which is why we should have taken more," Eshak said as he came to join the first guard.

"You know we can't afford to attract attention. The new Emperor has the Royal Fleet monitoring communications on this planet. Better to be discreet. Then we can return whenever we want."

"I say it's better to be bold. Fill up the ship, make a lot of credits, and retire." Eshak ran his eyes over the unconscious woman and licked his lips. "And if we took more, we could keep one for ourselves."

Kate shuddered. As appalling as she found the thought of being sold as a slave, the thought of being in the hands of someone as brutal as Eshak was just as bad.

"I hope this Royal Fleet locks you all up," she snapped.

Eshak reached through the bars with shocking speed, grabbing her dress and slamming her into the bars hard enough to knock the air out of her lungs. "You'd better hope not, human.

They're just as likely to throw you in prison for being on this ship. Or use you themselves."

The other guard gave him an odd look, then tugged Eshak away from the bars. "Come on. The captain wants to go over the inventory and decide on the best markets. It's a chance for you to tell him he's all wrong," he added sardonically.

Eshak actually seemed to flinch. "I'll pick my time," he muttered.

"Yeah, right."

The two of them disappeared down the corridor as Kate rubbed her aching chest.

"Are you all right?" Mary whispered.

"Just bruised. I never thought I would be grateful to be inside this cage, but at least he couldn't—" She broke off as she realized that something had changed. "Can you feel that?"

"Feel what?"

"The vibration. I think the ship is moving." She saw Mary's face pale as the other woman reached the same conclusion. "We're leaving Earth."

They sat in horrified silence as Kate let the foil flutter to the floor. She might possibly have been able to operate a transporter, but there was no way she could pilot a spaceship. Everything she had worked for was slipping away and she was powerless to stop it.

A harsh groan disrupted her gloom.

"Where the fuck am I?" The new woman sat up, rubbing her head. A stunning redhead, she glared fiercely at both of them. "And who the fuck are you?"

"Fellow captives," Kate said dryly.

"The headache doesn't last long." Mary gave the newcomer her usual cheerful smile.

"Aren't you a ray of fucking sunshine," the woman

muttered, then sighed. "I'm sorry. I've been having a bad week. A bad year, for that matter."

"That's all right," Mary said immediately. "Being kidnapped by aliens is enough to make anyone grouchy."

"Aliens?"

Her disbelief was clear, and Kate gestured at the other cages. "Take a look around."

"Fuck. I guess this week can get worse after all." A reluctant smile crossed her face. "I'm Lily, fellow captives."

It turned out that Lily ran a beach bar only one town away from Kate's lab. She'd been taken when she left the bar late at night.

"I had to close because I fired my bartender last week." Lily scowled. "Cheating bastard."

"I assume you had more than a professional relationship?" Kate asked dryly.

"Yeah. I know better, but man, did he look good naked."

She sighed wistfully, and Kate did her best to hide her skepticism. She'd never found the male body particularly aesthetically pleasing in real life.

Mary's eyes were as big as saucers. "I can't believe he cheated on you. You're beautiful!"

Lily grinned. "Thanks, sweetie. I just have shit taste in men."

"Me too," Mary said softly, a troubled look crossing her face before she smiled again. "What about you, Kate?"

She shrugged uncomfortably. "I don't really have time to date. But I'm sure if I did, the men would suck."

When the other two women laughed, she felt an unexpected sense of kinship. Mary had been right—this was better than being on her own.

The days settled into a monotonous routine, with little to differentiate them other than the regular feedings. Yakshi continued to come by periodically on his inspection rounds. He always gave Mary a treat, although he showed no interest in either Kate or Lily.

"I must be losing my appeal," Lily drawled after Yakshi dropped another bar in Mary's feed bowl before he hurried away.

"Maybe you should be a little nicer," Mary said, as she broke up the bar and passed them each a piece.

"In my experience, men only think one thing is *nice*, and I'm not prepared to go that far."

"Yakshi's not like that," Mary protested.

Lily let it drop in the face of Mary's distress, but she gave Kate a skeptical look. Kate suspected that Lily was quite right about Yakshi's intentions, even if he was only treating Mary like a cute little pet right now.

Kate estimated that they had been on board for approximately two weeks when Eshak suddenly appeared in front of her cage, unlocking it and dragging her out despite her panicked protests.

And now here she was, bobbing along in an alien ocean like a letter in a bottle. *Alone.* Her eyes unexpectedly filled with tears, but she refused to let them fall. She wasn't the type of woman who cried, and now was not the time to start. All she could do was hope that her friends' pods had landed safely, then do everything she could to find them.

Friends. It was almost as foreign a concept as aliens. She had been an awkward, gifted child—too smart for her own good, her dad used to say—and she had never been particularly close to anyone. But being confined, half-naked, in adjoining cages had created an unexpected bond. With little to do other than talk, she knew the other women better than she had ever known anyone.

Please let them be okay, she thought.

While she didn't worry as much about Lily—the fiery, determined redhead was a force to be reckoned with—Mary's innocent, optimistic nature would make her an easy target. Kate only hoped that Yakshi had been the one to take her to her pod.

But worrying about her friends wasn't going to help her escape the pod, and she had an uneasy feeling that time was not on her side. A small red light next to the door blinked rhythmically, and she remembered Yakshi's words about picking her up later. A tracking beacon of some kind? She most definitely did not want to be here when they returned.

At least her hands were free. The position was somewhat awkward, but she managed to reach the closure on the head restraint and gradually worked it open. Once she could move her head, it was easier to see the remaining fastenings and she opened them much faster. As she freed the last one, a large wave picked up the pod and slammed it down again, knocking her to the ground.

While she had been wrestling with the restraints, the sky had darkened, the two suns disappearing behind heavy clouds. Another wave caught the pod, and her stomach dropped as it rolled down the steep slope into the trough. Despite her feeling of urgency, if the storm was going to get worse, she would be better off staying safely in the pod until it passed.

That was when the first drop of water trickled through the seal around the door.

CHAPTER THREE

"Warden Pulata is waiting, Prince A'tai," Uauna murmured, coughing discreetly.

"What?" A'tai frowned, looking up from his desk. From the expression on his valet's face, it wasn't the first time he had spoken. "Can't it wait? I've just reached the most fascinating section on the influence of Namoan culture on the shipping routes between Kapenta and—"

"No doubt a very important factor at that time," Warden Pulata agreed, stepping into A'tai's study. "However, things have changed in the past two thousand years, and I believe the condition of the algae farms of Ataian is somewhat more urgent."

The presumption of the older male grated on A'tai's nerves, but Pulata was a dedicated House retainer. Despite his lack of respect, A'tai was quite sure he had the best interests of the House at heart. He sighed and focused on Pulata.

"There is no improvement?"

"We've lost another five percent over the past quarter." Pulata was Warden of the southern reaches of Maulimu territory, including the algae farms that were a primary source of trade. He took his responsibilities very seriously.

"But the remaining beds are still healthy and strong?"

"Yes," Pulata admitted.

"Then I am not sure why you believe this is so urgent."

"Because we have no answer as to why it occurs, and the damage continues to spread."

"It is still within the normal variations in yield, is it not?"

Pulata frowned. "Historically, yes. But not since we increased the efficacy of the nutrient mix. I really believe it would be beneficial for you to visit Ataian and see the damage for yourself."

A'tai swung his chair around to look out the open window at the gentle green waves of the ocean. They called to him, and he was tempted to agree to the journey. Ataian was one of his favorite places, and he would be free to explore the waters and pursue his research without any interruptions. But there were two upcoming meetings of the Historical Society, and his mother had informed him that his presence would be required at a banquet later this month. Which was almost enough to sway him into going, but she was invariably correct about these matters.

"This is not a convenient time for the trip," he said, turning back to face Pulata. "Perhaps later in the season."

"But, sire..."

"I will take your concerns under advisement."

"As your Warden, I really must insist—"

A'tai's patience ran out. He rose over the other male, allowing himself to tower just a little bit. "It is not your place to insist. I am Prince of House Maulimu. I have said that I will consider the matter. Now go."

Pulata bowed and left without another word. A'tai stared after him, a little ashamed of having lost his temper. He decided he would ask Uauna to set up another meeting with Pulata before he left the capital. He returned to his desk but before he could even pick up his scroll, Uauna appeared at the door again.

"Now what is it?" He did his best not to snap. Courtesy to his servants had been ingrained in him by his father—although it was not something his mother had ever shown any interest in enforcing.

"Your mother would like to see you, sire."

That was never good. He cast a wistful glance at the manuscript, but it was better to get it over with now. He wouldn't be able to concentrate anyway, wondering what she had in store for him.

The capital city of Kapenta was strung out across several islands, and the palace of Maulimu occupied a prime position on one of the inner islands. The building followed the gentle curve of the shoreline with his quarters at one end and his mother's at the other. He took the least populated route and did his best to look busy and unapproachable. That didn't stop him from being waylaid by a messenger from the chef wanting him to approve the menu for tonight's banquet—he didn't even remember that they were having a banquet—his chief guard, and three of the rather vapid females that his mother kept in her entourage. By the time he reached her quarters, his patience was worn thin.

"You sent for me?" he snapped. Civility to retainers was one thing, civility to the female who liked to torment him was a completely different matter.

"I'm so sorry. Did I interrupt your perusal of some ancient manuscript? I would have come to see you myself, but you know how uncertain my health can be. I really feel quite weak today," U'rsul murmured. She was posed languidly on a reclining couch positioned in the exact center of an immense bay window.

One of her females immediately rushed over to her with a golden cup of iced wine, while another proffered a damp, scented handkerchief. U'rsul gave them a faint, brave smile as A'tai did his best not to roll his eyes. His mother had enjoyed ill health for as long as he could remember—and he did mean *enjoyed* it. It allowed her to escape anything she considered unpleasant while miraculously permitting her to indulge in whatever activities appeal to her.

"You look fine to me, Mother. Positively blooming."

She gave him a reproachful look, but he could still see her preening under what she considered suitable praise. Praise that she undoubtedly deserved. She was still a remarkably attractive female, her smooth teal skin shimmering from perfumed oils rather than youth, but her limbs supple and graceful, and her golden eyes, so like his own, still large and bright.

"I do try to take care of myself, and not let my unfortunate weakness get the better of me. It's the least I can do in memory of your poor dear father. He did so like to see me looking my best."

Another statement that was undoubtedly true. His father had been madly in love with his mother, although A'tai often suspected that the emotion had not been returned. Although she had never married again after his father's death, and continued to wear the extremely flattering robes of the widow, he was well aware that she had not been faithful to his father's memory.

"Why did you send for me, Mother?"

Her gaze sharpened, and she waved a hand, dismissing her retinue. Once they were alone, she sat up, and the needle-sharp intelligence behind her fragile veneer appeared.

"I have been considering our position. It's time for you to choose a mate."

"What?" He wasn't sure what he'd been expecting—possibly an increase in her allowance or the proposition that they open a new trade route—but certainly not this. "I have no intention of choosing a mate anytime in the near future."

Or ever. He had seen the hold his mother had over his father, and he had no intention of allowing any female that same hold over him.

"Then you are not thinking logically." His mother rose gracefully and moved to the desk in the far corner of the room. Unlike all of the other elegant, delicate furniture which filled the room, her desk was a large, functional piece—although still built from rare pink coral and carved in intricate flourishes. She pulled up a holographic screen. "Look at this. Our revenue from the algae has not been increasing, despite the increase in prices."

He sighed and rubbed his neck. "You know that production is down. We are getting paid more, but for less product."

"None of our other ventures are showing increased profits either. Unless you are willing to let me open the gambling house I proposed—"

"How many times do I have to say no?"

For the first time an expression of irritation wrinkled her smooth features. "You're as stubborn as your father. With all the offworlders who come to the port, it would be immensely profitable."

"House Maulimu is not going to make a profit on the weakness of others."

"I suppose that means you would be no more amenable to opening a brothel? Very high-class, of course."

He stared at her in shock. It was the last thing he had expected to come out of her mouth. "Of course not."

"House Faleta opened one last quarter and it's the talk of the town."

Based on her wistful expression, she was more concerned about the fact that people were talking about another House than from actually profiting from such a venture.

"No, Mother."

"It's not profiting on the weakness of others. Unless you consider sexual attraction to be a weakness?"

He ignored the barbed tone. Although he was not immune to an attractive female, he had no desire to be led around by his moa, and his mating arm remained firmly under his control.

"I said no."

She shrugged gracefully, the movement causing her gossamer gown to shimmer in the soft light.

"Then you must choose a mate."

"I am not following your logic."

"The wealth of our House is not increasing, which means we are not growing. If we don't grow, we die. If you are unwilling to expand our business ventures, then the alternative is to merge our House with another House that can provide a new avenue of growth."

He rubbed his neck again and paced over to the open window. Her reasoning was somewhat convoluted, but it was not entirely false. His historical studies had shown time and time again that relaxing into complacency had a tendency to lead to the decline and eventually the fall of a great House. But marriage? There had to be another way.

"I suppose you have a mate already picked out?" he asked sardonically.

"I have two suggestions. Lady I'sua would bring all of the wealth and connections of House Ramata—"

"—which would in turn attempt to sublimate us to their interests."

"Exactly. It would be profitable but difficult to handle—especially if you continue to refrain from social gatherings."

That barb hit home. The balls, soirées, and banquets which occupied his mother's time were more than just the fashionable assemblies they appeared to be on the surface. Important information was exchanged and trades negotiated under the semblance of innocuous conversation. He had never enjoyed them and, after an obligatory season when he came of age, he had been quite content to leave it in his mother's capable hands. She might have been a coldhearted schemer, but she always had the best interests of the House at heart.

"I don't see that changing," he admitted.

"Then I propose a union with E'lofi of House Tiene," she said, shocking him again. House Tiene was newly formed from a rich merchant family, and from what he recalled, Lord F'tonu was a brash, loudmouthed male who very clearly showed his plebeian origins. He couldn't think of anyone less likely to appeal to his sophisticated mother. And as for E'lofi, he vaguely remembered her as a very shy, pretty debutante who had barely managed to speak a word to him the one time they had danced together.

"I must say you always manage to surprise me, Mother."

She shrugged again. "It's a logical choice. The family is wealthy, and they have excellent trade connections. F'tonu wants his daughter to move up in the world. She's pretty enough and better mannered than her father—and meek enough not to interfere with your chosen way of life."

That barb also sank home. He sometimes forgot that his mother knew him just as well as he knew her. It was true that he couldn't see little E'lofi attempting to interfere with his studies or make demands on his time...

Wait. Was he actually considering this? He suddenly felt the weight of the net closing around him and sprang to his feet.

His mother gave him the sharp-toothed smile of a deep sea predator. "I invited her to tea tomorrow afternoon so the two of you could meet. Quite informally, of course."

"I am devastated to have to miss that meeting, but I'm afraid that I will no longer be in the city."

"Why not?"

"I have to make a visit to the southern reaches and determine the issue with the algae production."

"Surely that can wait?" His mother sagged back against her couch reaching for one of her pill bottles. "Especially when you know that I am not feeling well."

"As you pointed out, if our production goes down, so does our wealth. And I know you wouldn't want that to happen." He hid a smile as a spike of annoyance flashed across her martyred expression, and bowed. "Perhaps when I return."

"When will that be?" Her voice floated after him, but he pretended not to hear as he hurried out of the room, already making plans.

He needed to get out of the palace, and he needed to get out now. Her next step would be to send her physician to talk to him about her precarious health, and if that didn't work, a parade of his counselors to try and convince him it was in the best interest of the House. He was quite capable of refusing all of them, but it would be unpleasant and tedious and because he believed his counselors had his best interests at heart, he would have to mind his manners. Best for everyone, if he was unable to be found.

He rang for Uauna as soon as he returned to his quarters. "Has Warden Pulata already left?"

"No, sire. I believe he has a meeting with Enetisi first."

Damn. The old scientist liked to talk, and he suspected it would not be a brief meeting. Uauna's tablet chimed, and he raised it to check the message.

"Physician Hollia is here to see you."

Just as he had predicted. He glanced at the open windows and made a quick decision.

"Please tell him that he just missed me, then pack a bag for me and give it to Warden Pulata. Tell him I will meet him on Ataian."

"Yes, sire. May I ask how you are intending to make your way there?"

"The old-fashioned way, of course." He grinned as he shucked his robe and headed for the window.

"But Prince A'tai..."

"Don't worry about me. I may even take some extra time to enjoy the journey."

Ignoring Uauna's shocked face, he dove out of the window and into the depths below. Despite the stringent rules governing the disposal of waste, the water around the city was cloudy and thick with the myriad scents of the population. No matter. He let his limbs unfurl, moving swiftly away from the congested area.

The cool water rushed across his skin, invigorating his senses. It had been far too long since he had indulged in the simple pleasure of the open ocean. Although he didn't think his mother was desperate enough to send someone after him, he kept well beneath the surface, allowing the currents and scents to guide him.

An hour passed before he finally rose to the surface to observe his surroundings. The Sisters—the two suns that usually filled the sky—had vanished beneath a thick covering of clouds. Darkness loomed on the horizon, and he caught the distant flash of lightning.

Damn. Open water was no longer quite so appealing.

He could weather the storm beneath the surface, but the currents would grow stronger and more turbulent as it neared.

He studied his surroundings again and spotted an outcropping of coral in the distance. If he remembered correctly, it was the formation known as the Tears of Latiti. It was riddled with caves, and he could wait out the storm there in relative peace.

He headed towards it, skimming along the surface of the water to make sure he remained on course. As he crested one of the rapidly swelling waves, he saw a foreign object in the distance—a spherical metal ball that looked like an escape pod from a spaceship. By the Sisters, what was that doing here?

If there had been an accident with one of the ships coming into port, then word would have been all over town. Perhaps it was just debris.

Curious, and a little annoyed that some captain might have polluted his waters, he headed for it. As he topped the next wave, he saw that the pod had settled lower in the water. The cheap vessel must have sprung a leak. Annoying, but perhaps for the best. Once it settled to the ocean floor, he could mark its location and send someone back to retrieve it. He was about to resume his original course when he saw a flutter of movement as the door began to open. A pale arm appeared in the narrow gap. It was occupied?

For a moment, he froze, and then he saw another wave break over it, rushing into the opening. The arm disappeared. *Fuck.* He dove beneath the surface and raced towards the pod.

He spotted it just as it sank beneath the waves completely. The person inside was still moving, fighting to pry open the heavy door but the weight of the water was against it. He swam even faster, but by the time he arrived, the occupant was barely moving. He wrenched open the door and found himself staring into two wide green eyes just before they fluttered shut.

Fuck.

He grabbed the female, yanking her out of the still descending pod. Pale, defenseless skin, no scales, no gills—she was not a creature of the sea. He snatched her up into his arms and headed for the surface, her body limp and unresisting. Rain had started to fall by the time he surfaced, but he did his best to shelter her, using his limbs to support her body as he forced the water from her lungs. She coughed just as a wave swept over them. The intensity of the storm was building. They couldn't remain on the surface.

He pressed his mouth against hers and forced it open, pulling water in through his gills and releasing oxygen into her mouth. For a moment, she fought him, but then she sighed into his mouth as her body softened, and he pulled them both back down below the waves.

Her mouth was unexpectedly delicious, her natural sweetness mingling with the salty tang of the ocean. He could feel her breathing in his oxygen, and he was suddenly conscious of the full, heavy weight of her breasts rubbing gently against his chest as her lungs filled. The only time a Mafanan female had engorged breasts was when she was with child, but he had seen enough offworlders to know that it wasn't true for all species. However, her species seemed to have particularly generous breasts.

In the past, he had considered such an enlargement to be rather unnecessary, disrupting the natural smooth lines of a female. But now that the soft mounds were pressed against his skin, the hard little points of her nipples an unexpectedly erotic counterpoint, he had an entirely different reaction. His mating arm stirred in its sheath, threatening to emerge, and he almost drew back in shock before he remembered that she needed his breath to survive.

Her legs drifted out next to him at an awkward angle, so he reached down to pull her closer. And found himself cupping a round, full ass, another trait so different from his people. His hand clenched involuntarily in the soft, ample flesh as he aligned her body with his. To his shock, her legs came up to curve around his waist as she clung to him. She was so close that he could feel the slippery heat of her cunt against his stomach, a shocking contrast to the cool water.

Her soft little tongue danced along his, as smooth as the finest silk, and his moa escaped his control and sprang free. He could taste her essence in the water, her sweetness washing over him, even more delicious than her mouth. His mating arm grew thicker as his limbs automatically moved into position, preparing to hold her open for him. But then she sighed into his mouth again with a soft little sound. Instead of resisting the mating like a Mafanan female, she seemed to nestle closer. It might just have been the action of the currents, but the unexpected gesture finally penetrated the haze of lust.

By the Sisters, what was wrong with him? He'd never had this type of reaction to a female before, and certainly not to an offworlder. Although she seemed to be encouraging him, he suspected that she was only partially conscious, dazed by the near tragedy. He would have to wait until he was sure she was awake. But perhaps then, if she was willing and his unnatural desire persisted...

His pace increased at the thought, heading for the Tears of Latiti with renewed urgency. Once there, she would no longer be reliant on him for oxygen and she would be free to choose him. His engorged moa throbbed painfully, and he swam deeper, hoping the cooler currents below would finally persuade it to return to its sheath. But then she shivered in his arms and he reversed his course. His unexpected protectiveness horrified him. Was he destined to repeat his father's mistakes after all?

No. She was a creature of the land. This could be no more than a temporary liaison. He had nothing more to offer.

CHAPTER FOUR

Kate swam in and out of consciousness, only vaguely aware of her surroundings, which seemed to change every time the darkness cleared momentarily. Her bed felt hard and uncomfortable beneath her, but then it was replaced by something soft and silky that cradled her aching body. The light changed from a cool, flickering green to a soft pink glow and back again.

Sometimes, a strong arm supported her as someone gave her careful sips of cool water. Other times, something rubbery and disgusting was pressed against her lips and she did her best to bat it away. Her arms felt weak and ineffectual, but apparently whoever was trying to feed her got the message.

The one consistent memory was a deep, rippling voice like water rushing over rocks. The voice soothed her, comforted her, and was always there. Golden eyes floated in and out of her vision, beautiful but alien, and something about them made her nervous. But then the voice would soothe her and a cool hand would stroke her burning head and she would slip peacefully back into the darkness.

But eventually, the illness passed and she awoke, fully aware of who she was—if not where she was. Her memories felt strangely distant, but she picked through them until she found the thread of her abduction. *Abduction.*

She started to surge to her feet, but her body was still too weak to obey her commands. As she collapsed back into her bed—bed?—she remembered the need for caution. Keeping her body still, she glanced around, her eyes widening as she took in her surroundings. Where the hell was she?

Instead of the white metal walls of the ship or the ragged interior of the escape pod, she saw what looked like an underwater cave. Dark green coral in fanciful shapes formed elaborate arches over her head. Tiny plants speckled the coral, glowing with a soft pink hue. To her left, the floor of the cave sloped down to an open pool with jade water lapping softly at the rock. To her right...

Her breath caught as she realized she was not alone. A man crouched next to a small depression in the rock. No, not a man. An alien.

She could see a broad, heavily muscled back, similar to human anatomy but covered in shimmering teal-colored skin. His hair was the same color—or perhaps it wasn't hair. The wide, wavy strands bore a definite resemblance to seaweed. Her heart skipped a beat.

Was he the one who had been taking care of her? It seemed to be the only logical premise, but why? Was he simply being compassionate? Or did he have something else in mind?

She frantically ran through her various aches, but there was nothing to suggest that he had molested her. How long would that last? The Ithyians had been quite clear that she and the others were to be sold for a very specific purpose. And since they had gone to the trouble of kidnapping them, there was obviously a market for human sex slaves.

The water looked temptingly close, but she didn't think she had the strength to swim away from that big, powerful body. But maybe she didn't need to. If she could get outside the cave and find a place to hide, she could return once he went in search of her. Then she could drink some of the water she could hear trickling down the wall. Her parched mouth eagerly endorsed the idea.

She started to edge cautiously towards the water but as soon as she moved, the silky strands that made up her bed rustled. The stranger turned towards her at once.

Golden eyes. The ones that had haunted her dreams. Huge, slit-pupiled, and utterly alien. For a moment, she felt trapped, drowning in those golden depths, then she snatched her gaze away. The rest of his features were not as striking. His nose and ears were flatter and more streamlined than those of a human, his mouth wider. Then he smiled and she saw his teeth —white, pointed, and sharp, more like those of a shark than a man.

Her stomach clenched and she tried to scramble towards the water, but her body still refused to obey. He frowned and quickly came to her side, moving with an odd gliding gait before bending down next to her.

"You must be still. Your body has not yet recovered its strength."

The deep, rippling voice washed over her and somehow calmed her panic. She took a deep breath, then another. However unlikely it seemed, maybe he was genuinely concerned for her wellbeing.

"Thir—thirsty," she croaked.

"Yes of course."

As he hurried back to the other side of the cave, she noticed that he was wearing very tight trousers, almost exactly the shade of his skin, that seemed to flow directly into odd shaped boots. Maybe that was the reason for his strange gait.

He returned almost immediately with a curved shell filled with water. She started to reach for it, but he put his arm behind her and lifted her into a sitting position against his shoulder. Part of her wanted to protest, but it felt oddly natural and she realized he must have been helping her drink like this while she was sick. She tried to reach for the shell cup, but her hand trembled so badly she couldn't clasp it. He put his hand over hers, long, cool fingers enclosing her much smaller digits, and lifted it to her mouth.

Two sips of cool liquid slid down her throat before he pulled it away.

"More." She tried to make it a demand, but it came out more like a plea.

"In a minute. If you drink too quickly, your body will reject it." Those disconcerting teeth flashed briefly. "Believe me, I have made that mistake."

The heat threatened to rise to her cheeks, but she sternly pushed aside her embarrassment. She wasn't responsible for her bodily reactions while she was ill. As they waited, he continued to hold her tucked against his chest. His skin felt cool and silky against her cheek, with a faint intriguing texture that was not quite scales but was definitely not human skin. This close to him, she was aware of just how much bigger his body was, but her panic hadn't reoccurred since he first spoke. His skin warmed slightly where they touched, and she became aware of a faint, tantalizing fragrance like the clean air after a storm.

To her horror, she realized she was sniffing him, seeking more of that intriguing scent. He moved slightly, restlessly, but didn't pull away. Instead, he gave her another few sips of water.

They lay heavily in her stomach for a moment, but they soon settled.

"Where am I?" she asked, her voice still hoarse. "What happened?"

"What do you remember?"

"I'm not really sure." Still not sure of his intentions, she kept her answer deliberately vague. "The pod landed in the ocean, but then it started to leak."

"Outdated equipment," he growled, his voice deepening. "You were lucky to even make it through the atmosphere. And even luckier that I saw you trying to escape."

"I didn't see a boat. What were you doing there?"

He shrugged a shoulder, and she actually felt his muscles rippling against her body. Wow. She didn't think she had ever been this close to somebody with such an impressive build. Maybe she shouldn't have been so quick to dismiss Lily's attraction to her cheating boyfriend. *Stay on track*, she scolded herself.

"I was swimming," he said casually.

"In a storm?"

He shrugged again, and she sternly ignored how good it felt.

"I did not expect a storm. I was in a hurry to leave the capital and rather foolishly did not check on the weather."

There was the faintest tinge of blue along his cheekbones. Was he embarrassed? The sight was unexpectedly reassuring, and she found herself smiling up at him.

"I'm Kate, by the way."

"And I am Pr—I am A'tai. At your service."

She was quite sure that if he hadn't been holding her, he would have bowed. Apparently, not all aliens were as uncouth as her captors. But the thought of them reminded her of her friends, and she tried to struggle upright.

"I wasn't alone. There were two more of us. Did you see any other pods? Any other humans?"

He helped her sit up, but he kept his arm around her back, a cool, reassuring band of muscle.

"I'm afraid not. But my focus was on rescuing you from the storm."

"And I really appreciate that, but is there a way—"

She stopped abruptly. He had been very nice to her, but he was still a stranger. Did he realize that she was going to be sold as a slave? What if whoever he communicated with wasn't as nice? She didn't want to put Mary and Lily in danger.

"A way to communicate with the surface?" He finished for her. "I do not have a communicator with me."

"What do you mean surface? And how do you know it's still storming? How long have we been here?"

"To answer your questions in order, first, we are in one of the underwater caves beneath the Tears of Latiti." He held up a long finger and she saw in fascination the webbing between his digits. "Two, rainwater continues to trickle down from above so the heavens are still open. That is what you are drinking, by the way. And finally, we have been here for three days."

"I've been sick for three days?" Her shoulder sagged and she felt him pull her back against his chest. Even if her friends had landed nearby, the storm would have sent them a long distance away by now. She could only hope that their pods had been more watertight than hers.

"You almost drowned." His fingers fleetingly caressed her cheek. "And I suspect you were not well before then."

He was probably right. She had eaten little on the ship; none of them had. How was she going to find the others? "When will the storm end?"

"At this time of year, I would not expect it to last for more than another day. Two at the most." He frowned down at her.

"But I will not be able to obtain any surface foods for you until it stops. You need to regain your strength, but you refused the mollusks I tried to give you. Is there anything from beneath the water that you can eat?"

"I can eat fish," she said unenthusiastically. It had never been one of her favorites, but she was sensible enough to know that he was right. A wave of exhaustion swept over her and right now, sleep seemed a lot more appealing than food. He gave her a little more water, but her eyes refused to stay open, and with a tired sigh, she turned her face to the firm muscles of his chest and went to sleep.

A'TAI STARED DOWN AT THE FEMALE SLEEPING SO trustingly in his arms. Despite her disastrous landing and her obvious weakness, she had not complained. He could only imagine how his mother would have reacted in the same situation.

The impulse to protect her still concerned him. His father had always been overly concerned with his mother's welfare, and he was determined not to follow in his footsteps. *I should put her down*, he told himself, but he did not want to release her. His gaze drifted down over the white slave gown that barely concealed her curves. Perhaps there was another way.

The subject of slaves had been under much discussion in the Empire recently, with rumors flying around that the new Emperor would outlaw the practice. However, it was such an intrinsic economic factor in many of the worlds that made up the Empire that such a ruling could create outright rebellion. To date, the new Emperor had only focused on making sure that the existing laws protecting slaves were fully enforced. Under those laws, abandoning a slave in a faulty escape pod would constitute negligence. He would be completely justified in removing her from her owner and assuming responsibility.

Although slavery was not a common practice on Mafana, neither was it forbidden. If he took ownership, then he would be fully justified in his desire to protect her. But as his slave, she would not be able to manipulate him the way his mother had manipulated his father. The more he thought about the idea, the more it appealed to him. She would belong to him, and only to him. He would not have to take her to balls or any other tedious social events. He would never have to worry about her cheating on him.

He would not demand a physical relationship, of course, but if he was a good master and treated her with great care, there was no reason why she would not come to welcome the idea.

His eyes drifted back down over the white shift. It was designed to accentuate a slave's assets and make it easy for their masters to access them. Even now, it had slipped apart to reveal the lush curve of her hip and a tantalizing glimpse of the small patch of fur between her legs. If someone had asked him three days ago, he would have found the idea distasteful, but now the dark silky curls that veiled her little pink cunt were as provocative as the white shift.

His moa pressed against his sheath again and he swore. He had done his best to ignore her tantalizing body as he cared for her. He had been reasonably successful when her illness was at its height and his concern outweighed his unfortunate desire, but now that she was clearly on the road to recovery, his neglected moa was reasserting itself.

He forced himself to settle her back in the bed of soft sea grasses, averting his eyes as a rosy little nipple peeked out from the edge of her gown. The most important thing right now was to restore her health. Since she had said she would eat fish, he would descend into the deep, cold waters beneath them to hunt for the delicacies that swam there. Hopefully the cold water would also relieve his rampant moa. But as he slipped into the water and unfurled his limbs, he suspected it was a useless hope.

CHAPTER FIVE

When Kate woke the second time, she no longer felt as dizzy and confused. Her body still ached and her strength hadn't returned, but she knew who she was and where she was. She searched for A'tai and found him crouched against the wall again, collecting the water that trickled down the rocks into the shell cup.

"Hello," she said softly as she tried to sit up.

He was at her side immediately, supporting her with a strong arm as he offered her another drink. This time he didn't object when she sipped more, although she did her best to take it slowly.

"Do you feel better?" His golden eyes scanned her face, obviously concerned, and she managed a smile.

"I do. I just wish I wasn't so weak."

"You must eat," he said firmly. "I hunted a narifa for you. Its flesh is much prized. Can you sit without my support?"

"Apparently not." As soon as he started to pull away she swayed dizzily.

He frowned thoughtfully, then lifted her as if she weighed

no more than a ragdoll and carefully positioned her with her back against the cave wall. The strength in his arms, the ease with which he maneuvered her, and the tantalizing scent that rose from his skin caused an unexpected ache low in her stomach. She almost regretted it when he let her go.

He hovered close to her for a moment, checking on her stability, and she found herself staring into his eyes. The mysterious pools of gold seemed to call to her, and her gaze dropped to his mouth, wide and full with surprisingly sensual lips. She was almost tempted to lean closer before she came to her senses and quickly looked away.

"This is fine, thank you."

He lingered for another fraction of a second, then turned and glided back across the cave. Why did he walk so differently, she wondered, trying to distract herself. What were his feet like in those odd-looking boots?

Before she could decide, he returned carrying a thin slab of rock, with strips of white fish artfully arranged on the surface. They looked surprisingly tempting. Perhaps this wouldn't be so bad after all. She reached for one but as her fingers closed around it, she realized it was cool to the touch. Raw. Damn. She should have realized that there was nowhere to build a fire.

"It's quite fresh," he assured her.

"Umm, I'm sure it is. It's just..."

"You must eat in order to regain your strength. Do you want to try the mollusks again?"

His words brought up the memory of something rubbery being pressed against her mouth, and she shuddered.

He gave her a worried frown. "You said you would eat fish. Is there another kind that you prefer?"

What she really wanted was a nice juicy hamburger, but that was obviously not an option. And he was right, she did need to eat. *Just think of it as sushi,* she told herself, even though she'd never really cared for sushi either.

She reluctantly lifted the piece of fish to her mouth, then swallowed it as fast as she could before she could taste it. To her surprise, it didn't even leave an unpleasant, fishy aftertaste.

"Take another," he urged.

The second time was easier, and this time she cautiously bit down on the fish. It practically melted in her mouth, slightly salty but with a faint trace of sweetness.

"This is very good," she told him, and he nodded with satisfaction.

"I told you it was a delicacy. The hunt is difficult, and not many choose to go after it." A faint hint of blue washed over his features. "But we are fortunate in being close to its territory."

"Where did you say we were? Are we near your capital city?"

"The Tears of Latiti. We are some distance from Kapenta." He gave her an odd look, then asked slowly. "Are you familiar with Mafana?"

"No, I—"

"I suspected as much." He rose and started pacing. "Your owner was most remiss in abandoning you here in a damaged pod."

"My owner?" Her heart sank. Despite his kindness, he obviously thought of her as nothing more than a slave. Did that mean he would return her to the Ithyians? The thought made her lose her appetite, and she pushed away the remaining fish.

"I have a proposition," he said, his voice stiff. "It is acceptable under Imperial law to remove a slave from an owner who mistreats her. If you agree, I will assume responsibility for you."

So much for his kindness. *He's just as bad as the aliens who abducted me,* she thought bitterly. But then she forced herself to push aside her resentment and consider the situation. He had saved her life, cared for her while she was ill, and seemed concerned for her wellbeing. As far as she could tell, he had not molested her. That put him head and shoulders above the Ithyians.

As much as she resented the idea, if she was now in a world where slavery was legal, a kind master was certainly better than the alternative. And he had mentioned laws covering his behavior...

"What are the laws about slavery?"

"You do not know?" His teeth flashed, but this time it was most definitely not a smile. "You should have been informed. There are some finer points, but essentially a slave must be provided with adequate food, adequate clothing, and adequate shelter. They are not allowed to be abused."

She suspected that *adequate* was open to interpretation, but she was more focused on the last statement.

"What counts as abuse? Does that include sexual relationships?"

A tide of pale blue washed over his face and down his chest.

"A sexual relationship is permitted if it is consensual," he said, even more stiffly.

"So if I say no?"

"I would never force you."

He looked appalled at the suggestion, but then again, he hadn't denied his interest.

"You give me your word?"

The horror changed to indignation. "I am a Pr—member of the House of Maulimu. My word is sacred."

She considered him thoughtfully. The very fact that he had asked was a point in his favor. Given the ease with which he had lifted her earlier, he would have had no trouble forcing himself on her. He had mentioned the capital earlier. She suspected it would be the best place to try and seek news of her friends. If she agreed to this charade—temporarily—until they traveled there...

"Do you require my consent to... belong to you?"

He shrugged a shoulder. "Not technically. But I wish to be clear."

"Is there anything else you want to clarify?"

"I will provide for you in all things and protect you against all others. I will treat you with the utmost respect. You will belong only to me." He hesitated, then looked her directly in the eyes. "But since you asked for clarity, I find you very desirable. I intend to have you in my bed. When you are ready."

Her breath caught at the intensity on his face. No human man had ever looked at her with such desire, and part of her responded instinctively. She felt her nipples tighten against the silky fabric of her dress, and saw his eyes drop to them. Gold flickered across his skin. His hunger was almost palpable, but he didn't move towards her, and more than anything, that decided it for her.

"Very well."

He took one step in her direction, and her heart started to pound, not entirely from fear. Had she misjudged him?

But instead of continuing across the cave, he whirled and dove into the open water, disappearing beneath the surface without a sound.

"I didn't expect that," she said to the now silent cave.

As she waited for him to return, she finished off the last of the fish and drank some more water. The combination left her feeling unexpectedly content, and she wiggled back down into her bed. She had every intention of watching out for his return, but her body betrayed her and she was asleep long before his head emerged from the water.

. . .

A'TAI SWAM DEEPER INTO THE CHILLY DEPTHS, FIGHTING the urge to return to Kate. But the triumph that had roared through him at her consent had also resulted in his moa threatening to emerge.

He shook his head in disgust and went deeper. He had assured her that he would not take advantage of her submission, but as soon as she agreed to his ownership, he had wanted nothing more than to wrap her in his limbs and explore every inch of that strange, tempting body.

Ownership. He tested the word on his tongue—it sounded both perfect and yet somehow wrong. He preferred to think that she belonged to him, that she had chosen to belong to him. And that she had made that decision without knowing that he was the Prince of House Maulimu. He wasn't quite sure why it mattered so much to him, but he liked knowing she had made her decision without that knowledge.

He remembered the way she had looked into his eyes as she agreed, the way her ridiculously large breasts had quivered beneath her gown, and suddenly realized that he was swimming back towards the cave. *Fuck.* He had given her his word. He had promised to provide for her and to protect her... He came to an abrupt halt, floating in the water as he remembered his exact words. They were the same words exchanged in a bonding ceremony.

Don't be foolish, he told himself as he resumed swimming. They didn't—couldn't—apply to a slave in the same way. They must have been in his mind because of his mother's insistence on him taking a mate.

And yet... they had seemed exactly right when he was saying them.

As much as he hated to admit that his mother was right, perhaps he needed to find a mate after all. Not that he had any intention of giving up Kate. But he was getting ahead of himself. Right now, his only concern should be whether or not the storm continued to rage.

He stroked up to the surface to check on its progress. The water still rose and fell in angry swells but the skies were beginning to clear. The Elder Sister was setting in a blaze of angry red, her smaller Sister following behind as always.

No more than another day perhaps, and they would be able to move on. But where would they go?

The thought of returning to the palace did not please him. While he might be prepared to acknowledge the possibility of a bonding ceremony, he was in no hurry to move forward with it. The palace on Ataian was equally unappealing. He would be forced to resume his official duties. Although, at least he would be able to make sure that Kate was fed and clothed as befitted his companion.

Companion...

He owned a small property on the unpopulated side of Ataian. His old nurse and her husband had retired there and kept an eye on the property while managing a small farm. The presence of another female would undoubtedly reassure Kate, and Simea had never treated him as royalty. It was the perfect solution.

When he returned to the cave, he found Kate asleep, her pale skin flushed pink in the glow of the susulu. She looked so delicate, so ethereal, that he wanted to touch her to make sure that she wasn't going to vanish.

But no, he had promised. A wave of fatigue tugged at him. He had spent most of the past three days caring for Kate and the lack of sleep was catching up with him. He eyed the bed he had created. Would he be breaking his vow to share it with her?

No, he decided. He could even argue that it was his bed and he was allowing her to share it with him. He eased down next to her, careful to maintain some distance between their bodies to appease his insistent conscience.

His good intentions were immediately thwarted when she rolled over and snuggled against his side. Her soft, warm curves pressed against him, and his limbs started to unfurl, to pull her more tightly into his embrace. He gritted his teeth and refused to let them. But neither did he move her away—she had turned to him and he was breaking no vow to allow it. He let the tantalizing warmth of her touch carry him into slumber.

CHAPTER SIX

Kate was dreaming. She was in her lab, studying the latest sample from the coast, when a man came up behind her and wrapped his arms around her waist. Big, powerful arms, but she wasn't afraid. Instead, she leaned against him, knowing he would support her. His scent surrounded her, reminding her of the sea water she was analyzing.

He remained there as she added a drop of reagent to the latest sample, and she didn't mind. That was another reason she knew it had to be a dream—she hated having anyone around when she was deep in an experiment. Even though her brain was focused on the changes in the sample, her body hummed pleasantly with the awareness of his presence.

When her work was completed, he would be waiting for her. She put her hand on his arm, and even in her dream she realized something was different. His arm was long and firm and smooth, but it didn't contain the musculature she expected. More curious than afraid, she ran her fingers along the edge and discovered small suckers that clung gently to her skin as if kissing her.

As she explored, the not-arm came up to brush across her breast, pressing small, sucking kisses to the sensitive mound. Arousal washed over her so quickly that it shocked her awake.

And discovered she wasn't dreaming.

A giant tentacle was wrapped around her waist, the tip curling up onto her breast. Oh my God. Something must have crawled up out of the opening in the cave floor. Was it going to pull her back into the water? Forcing herself to breathe slowly and calmly, she tried to slide out from under it, but as soon as she moved it tightened around her. The grip wasn't in the least painful—in fact, it felt disturbingly erotic as it tightened around her breast—but it was clear that it had no intention of letting her go.

The rest of her body was pressed up against A'tai. He wasn't moving, so he must still be asleep. Since they were in his territory, hopefully he had some idea of how to deal with the creature.

"A'tai," she whispered, then paused to wonder if the tentacled creature could hear. When neither one reacted, she tried again, louder this time. "A'tai!"

He sprang into wakefulness, moving in front of her with shocking speed. As he did, the tentacle disappeared and she breathed a sigh of relief.

Until she realized that it had reappeared under A'tai, along with several more. For a horrified moment, she thought it was attacking him, and then she saw that his legs had disappeared, replaced by tentacles.

"What is it?" he demanded, scanning the cave. "Did something threaten you?"

"You—you're part octopus." Her voice came out shaky and

breathless, even as part of her mind was immediately sidetracked by curiosity as to what type of evolutionary path had led to this.

"I don't understand. There is no danger?" He looked confused, but after another glance around the empty cave, he lifted his body into a standing position. His tentacles wound together and formed what looked like human legs as he hurried back to her side.

"How do you do that?" she asked.

"Assume a land form?" He actually looked confused. "Is this not common in your world? Like this octopus you mentioned?"

"Umm, no. It's a sea creature with tentacles, but much smaller. And not intelligent." *Although they had shown significant puzzle-solving skills.*

His confusion turned to outrage. "You are comparing me to a lower life form?"

"Of course not. But perhaps there was some common ancestry. Or I mean, there would have been if you had been on Earth." She glared at him. "You have to give me a minute here. We don't have people who change forms, except in fairy tales." And some of the romance stories she read late at night.

"I see." He sank down on his knees beside her. *Not knees*, she reminded herself, even though the movement looked remarkably similar.

"You said this was your land form. Why did you switch while you were sleeping?"

"I did?"

"You most certainly did. I went to sleep with a man and woke up with a tentacle around my... waist." She could feel her cheeks heating, but decided not to mention where else his tentacle had ended up.

The pale blue she had noticed before flickered across his skin. Definitely embarrassment, she decided, remembering that octopi could change color in regards to stimuli. What other reactions might he have? She suddenly remembered the gold that had shimmered across his skin just before he left her the previous day. What did it mean?

"I apologize if I startled you." He seemed sincere, but she noticed he didn't attempt to explain why the transformation had occurred.

"You can choose to use either form?" Now that she was over her initial shock, a number of questions bubbled up.

"Of course. The transformation is instinctive, but I can always control it if I wish."

"That's fascinating. Is there an evolutionary reason for the two forms?"

He sat back on his... feet and smiled at her. Those sharp pointed teeth made more sense now.

"There is a legend. Matua, the Elder Sister, created us from the sea foam as it sparkled in her rays. But Latiti, the Little Sister, was jealous and wanted us to visit her land, so she gave us the ability to form legs and breathe air."

"That doesn't exactly strike me as a scientific explanation," she said dryly.

"Perhaps not, but it is a more interesting explanation than the fact that the ability to adapt to both environments undoubtedly provided a better chance for survival."

"Maybe you're right," she laughed. "May I see?"

She extended her hand without really thinking about it, but saw his body tense. Instead of responding verbally, he simply uncurled a single tentacle and offered it to her. The movement was so graceful and natural that she didn't find it alarming, especially since he simply held it out and waited for her to touch him.

A little cautiously, she stroked her hand along the back. It felt almost identical to the skin on his chest, just slightly rougher, the texture more obvious here. But when she slipped her hand underneath, the skin there was velvety soft. A row of equally soft, flexible suckers ran down each side—which technically made them limbs rather than tentacles. As she brushed across the suckers, she felt him shiver and looked up to find him watching her, his face intense.

"Are they sensitive?"

"Yes."

"I'm sorry. I didn't mean to hurt you -"

"You're not hurting me," he said firmly, curling the limb around her hand.

One of his suckers pressed against her palm in what felt like a kiss, and it was her turn to shiver. Why did that feel so good? Her fingers closed around him, and she saw that wash of gold flicker over his skin. Hmm. Purely in the interest of science, she tightened her grip, then dragged her hand down to the narrow tip, letting her fingers trail across the underside.

He groaned, and the gold became more distinct before he pulled away from her, tucking his limb back in place.

"You taste delicious," he said. "But if you want me to keep my promise, I think it's time to end this exploration."

"I was just testing your response to stimuli," she said, hoping that she wasn't blushing. But then she thought back to his words the last time she'd been awake. "You said you wanted a physical relationship with me."

A definite flicker of gold. "Yes."

"Is that even possible? Given our... differences?"

"Oh yes. I assure you I can pleasure you."

His eyes gleamed with hunger, and she felt an unexpected pulse in her long-neglected clit as she imagined those small sucking kisses all over her body. For once, she had no response.

For a long moment they stared at each other, and she could see his skin shimmer. But then he shook his head, and turned away.

"You are dangerous to my self-control, amali."

"Amali?"

"A type of coral. Soft and beautiful—and deadly."

That was actually rather flattering. It made her feel like some type of femme fatale instead of boring old Kate. She smiled at him. "I guess I'll take that as a compliment."

"You should." He glided over to the water. "Now I must check on the storm. And perhaps more fish?"

As delicious as the fish had been, the thought of a steady diet of it didn't thrill her. But it would have to do until they reached land. A sudden thought struck her.

"When we leave here, where are we going?"

"To one of the southern islands. I have a... home there."

"On the surface?"

He laughed. "Yes. My people spend most of their time there. Latiti was right about the lure of the land."

That part was a relief, but an island sounded kind of isolated. "Is the capital on the island?"

"No. You do not need to worry. It is very quiet and isolated."

With a reassuring smile, he slipped into the water. She scrambled over to the hole just in time to see all of his limbs gracefully unfurl before he disappeared from sight. With a sigh, she sat back. Normally a quiet island would have sounded wonderful, especially if the slavers were looking for her, but if she was that isolated, how could she gather information about this world? And more importantly, how could she find her friends?

A'tai did seem very intrigued by her—and concerned about pleasing her. Maybe it was just because she was different, but if she could take advantage of that interest, convince him she wanted to see the capital…

She'd never even considered using her feminine wiles on a man before, but then again, A'tai wasn't exactly a man. And the thought of becoming more intimate with him wasn't exactly unpleasant. Her traitorous body definitely agreed. A speculative smile curved her lips as she went to collect more water.

CHAPTER SEVEN

Seems I am destined to spend all of my time around Kate with my moa threatening to emerge, A'tai thought ruefully as he swam away from the cave. Just the memory of her soft little fingers stroking his suckers made it throb. When she had asked him if they were compatible, her eyes so wide and green, he had been on the verge of showing her exactly how well their bodies would fit together.

But then a flicker of doubt crossed his mind. He had seen enough while he cared for her to know that her cunt was as small and delicate as the rest of her, and his moa was not small. He would have to prepare her well before holding her in the mating position. The thought of that preparation made him throb again, and he forced his mind back to more practical matters.

Kate seemed anxious to be on land once more, so he would check the condition of the waves first. He emerged to find that both suns had risen. Long, rolling swells surrounded him but they would be easy enough to navigate, even on the surface. The trip to Ataian would take no more than a few hours, so he decided not to stop and fish. Simea would have plenty of food for them.

As he surfaced in the cave pool, he saw Kate standing by the far wall of the cave, using the thin trickle of fresh water to bathe. He froze as he watched her wipe a wet hand across her neck, then down under the short gown to trace her breasts. His moa jerked against his sheath when her hand started to descend further, and he forced himself to interrupt.

"We have bathing facilities at my home."

She jumped, but then she turned to face him. The dampness made the thin material cling to those intriguing breasts, and he could see every detail, even the impudent peaks pressing against the fabric. He ached to explore those tempting little buds, to find out if they were as delicious as the rest of her skin, but he confined himself to a visual exploration. Somewhat to his surprise, she let him look. Although the pink glow of the susulu made it difficult to know for sure, he could have sworn that her color had deepened. Was that a sign of her arousal?

But then she twisted her hands together and he saw them tremble. No, she wasn't ready. He would have to be satisfied with the fact that she seemed to be adjusting to him.

"The seas have calmed," he said as he rose into the cave and assumed his land form. "This would be a good time to resume our journey."

"To your island?"

"Yes."

"How far is it? I can swim, but it's been a long—"

"I will carry you," he said firmly. He would not permit her fragile body to be at the mercy of the water.

"Won't I be too heavy?"

He forced himself not to be insulted at her assumption of his weakness. She was still new to their ways. "Not in the least. But..."

"But what?"

"This cave is quite a long way beneath the water. In order to rise slowly and carefully to the surface, we will need to share breath."

"What does that mean?"

"I will take in oxygen through my gills and breathe it into your mouth."

"You have gills?" Her uncertainty vanished as she inspected him curiously. "Of course. That makes perfect sense now that I think about it. May I see?"

He made himself stand still as she approached and raised her hand to his neck. A male's gills were his weakest point—if an enemy clawed them open, he would be unable to breathe beneath the waters. In the old days, only the most vicious fighters would dare such a move. But this was Kate, and he breathed in her tantalizing fragrance as she brushed her soft fingers along the fragile slits No one had ever touched him there before, and a sudden bolt of unexpected lust washed over him.

Her eyes widened. "Does that feel good?"

"They are sensitive," he said noncommittally as he gently drew her hand away. "Are you ready?"

Her lips twisted. "It's not like I have anything to pack."

She would soon, he vowed. Clothes and jewels that suited her exotic beauty.

"Put your arms around my neck." He leaned down and scooped her up. The exquisite softness of her body pressed against his distracted him to the point where he almost missed her nervous gasp. "Don't worry. I won't let anything happen to you."

"Are you sure this is going to work?"

Her face was so close to his, her eyes wide and scared. He put his arm beneath her round little bottom, pulling her closer to him. To his delight, her legs came up and encircled his waist, her sweet little cunt pressed against his stomach.

"I'm sure. This is how I brought you here. Just hold on to me and put your mouth against mine."

Her little pink tongue swiped across her lips, and then she obeyed. He gently pushed her lips further apart until he could breathe into her mouth. To his shock, her tongue flicked against his, soft and smooth and delicious. Did she remember exploring him that way when he carried her to the cave? But this time he knew she was conscious, and with a groan, he let himself explore in return.

She clung to him, just as she had done before, and his limbs started to unfurl. One came up to curve under her ass, tasting the soft curves. It wasn't until another started to curl around her leg and he realized that he was on the verge of putting her into the mating position that he came to his senses. He made himself raise his head.

Her eyes as dark as the stormy sea, she stared up at him. Her lips were damp and swollen, impossibly tempting, but she spoke before he could taste them again.

"I-I thought we were leaving."

"We were. Until you kissed me."

Even in the pink glow, he was sure her cheeks grew darker.

"I was... curious. Your tongue—you have suckers there as well?"

"Yes. Does it disturb you?"

She shivered, and he could feel the hard points of her breasts pressing against him like heated pebbles. "No. But maybe we should actually leave this time?"

"Then as soon as our mouths touch, I will take you into the water—before we are distracted again. Do not be afraid, amali."

She nodded and he pressed his mouth to her once more, and dove.

KATE AND THE KRAKEN

. . .

Kate fought back an immediate sensation of panic as the water closed over them. Her arms and legs were wrapped so tightly around A'tai she was surprised he could move, but he didn't even pause. His limbs flared out beneath her, expanding and contracting in a rhythmic pulse that drove them through the water with astonishing speed. His mouth was still pressed to hers, and after her initial panic faded, she could feel the faint rush of oxygen into her lungs.

As she relaxed, she thought back to their kiss. She really had been curious, and still trying to decide if she could be the seductive type, when she stroked her tongue against his. But then he had responded and all thoughts of seduction flew out of her mind. All she could do was hold on as he took over. And that tongue—teasing, sucking, setting her nerves quivering with excitement. Her nipples had tightened, and she could actually feel herself dampen. She had been on the verge of writhing against him when he lifted his head.

The only thing that had stopped her from melting with embarrassment was that he was clearly equally aroused. His skin was flushed gold, and she was sure that one of his limbs had been curled around her butt, pressing those soft, sucking little kisses to the sensitive flesh. What would they feel like against other, even more sensitive areas? The image sent a fresh rush of arousal to her core and he jerked against her.

How could he possibly know she was aroused? And yet, she was sure that she had seen the flicker of gold across his skin.

Determined to divert her mind, she turned her attention to the surrounding water. Despite the jade green tint, it was remarkably clear. A variety of brightly colored fish and plants surrounded them. Even though she had specialized at a microscopic level, she recognized the signs of a vibrant and healthy ocean. Although they were moving swiftly through the water, there was an almost hypnotic quality to their journey, and she found herself relaxing into A'tai's arms as he swam.

When he finally breached the surface, the air on her face felt strange, and it took a moment before she thought to pull away from his mouth. He smiled at her.

"Is this better?"

She took a deep breath of the warm, salty air, then smiled back. "In some ways. But I... I enjoyed our journey."

"As did I. But I think we can accomplish the rest of the journey on the surface, unless the waves increase."

As far as she could tell, nothing surrounded them but endless rolling green waves. If she'd been on her own, she would have been terrified. But A'tai's presence put her at ease. She was quite sure he would take care of her.

"How do you know which way to go? Because of the suns?"

"Somewhat. But more from the feel and taste of the currents."

Wasn't that an octopus trait as well? The ability to taste with their suckers? *No wonder he sensed my arousal,* she thought, her cheeks heating.

He didn't seem to notice, adjusting their position so that they were horizontal in the water. He still kept her cradled against his chest as he started swimming again, and she noticed that he kept his head positioned to shield her from the oncoming waves. The sky overhead was a pale aqua, gradually lightening as the last of the storm clouds blew away.

Even though her work revolved around the ocean, she rarely made it out on the water anymore, and she realized she had missed it. She relaxed against him, watching sleepily as the water rushed by and birds circled far overhead, content to let him carry her across the water.

CHAPTER EIGHT

A'tai was almost sorry when Ataian came into view. He loved the island and had always felt at home here, but it also meant that he would no longer have Kate in his arms. He had never realized that carrying a female through the water could be such a pleasurable, sensual experience. By Mafanan tradition, the initial mating of a bonded couple occurred in the ocean, but, driven by their biology, the females always resisted. The mating position had developed as a way to hold them in place.

But Kate did not resist him. Instead she clung to his body, her soft curves a constant temptation. She wouldn't fight him—couldn't fight him—if he spread her open and let his mating arm seek the slick warmth of her cunt. The thought sent another wave of arousal over his body and once again, his moa pressed against his sheath. Perhaps he should cover her mouth with his and seek the cooling waters below—but he somehow suspected that it would only add to his arousal. And he had promised her not to touch her against her will.

He contented himself with slowing his pace and taking the

longer way around the right side of the island. This also meant he could avoid traveling past the small palace that perched on the southernmost tip. He still found himself reluctant to divulge his identity. Although she had already agreed to belong to him, he knew from past experience that people changed once they found out about his heritage. And he did not want her to change. He enjoyed her lack of obeisance, her boundless curiosity, and her obvious intelligence...

His strokes slowed even more as he remembered her questions in the cave. She seemed to possess a level of knowledge that was unusual in a slave. If she had been specially trained, then she would be even more valuable, and it was more likely that someone would come to claim her.

No! She was his.

No matter who had owned her before, they had not cared for her properly, and now she belonged to him. He didn't realize that his arms had tightened around her until she uttered a muffled protest and wiggled in his arms. Her struggle triggered an instinctive response. One limb came up to wrap around her wrists while two others automatically clasped her legs and began to separate them.

"A'tai?"

Her soft whisper penetrated his possessive haze, and he looked down to find her watching him, sea green eyes wide. He immediately relaxed his grip, and yet... her nipples were burning points against his chest, and he tasted an incredible sweetness in the water between them. Was she aroused by his actions?

"Did you like that?"

Under the clear light of the Sisters, there was no mistaking the tide of pink that washed across her face. Fascinating. It appeared that her species was not as different from his own as he had imagined.

"N-No. I mean, I don't know. I've never had anyone hold me down like that before."

Satisfaction roared through him. "Good."

Her chin lifted. "I suppose you do it all the time."

"I have never restrained a female in the mating position," he growled. His few liaisons had occurred on land and had not involved his moa. They had been driven by curiosity as much as desire.

"Mating position? But—"

"Our destination is ahead," he interrupted, swinging around so she could see the lush blues and greens of the island rising out of the waters. He wasn't ready to have this conversation.

"It's beautiful. What is it called?"

"Ataian."

"That's pretty." Her little brows drew together. "It sounds like your name."

"That is because I was named after it." As was every first son of the House of Maulimu. The island was their ancestral home.

They were close enough now to see the small cluster of white buildings perched on the rocks next to the wide beach, and contentment filled him. He loved the whole island, but this simple farmhouse had always felt most like home to him.

"This is where you live? Not in the capital?"

It was not the first time she had mentioned Kapenta. He had thought her concern was avoiding it, but perhaps there was more to her questions. Did she fear city life or did she enjoy it? Had her former owner paraded her beauty around in front of others? He would never do such a thing.

"Do you enjoy social activities?" he asked cautiously.

"Me? God, no. I spend most of my time work—I mean, pleasing my master."

She gave him an innocent look, running her tongue across her lips, and although his moa jerked at her last words, he suspected her original statement had been more accurate.

"I travel there occasionally," he admitted. "Although, like you, I prefer working."

She looked adorably confused, and he relented. "Perhaps we can take a trip there. When the time is right."

Which would most certainly not be until he was sure she was entirely his.

He could almost see the question of "when" rising to her lips, but he directed her attention back to the approaching land. An imposing figure had appeared on the beach, and he bit back a smile. Of course Simea knew he was coming.

"It looks as though Simea is already waiting for us."

"Who is she?"

"My old nurse," he said automatically, then winced. Still, surely it wasn't that uncommon for a family to hire someone to look after their child. "When she retired, she and her mate decided to stay on as caretakers."

"That's nice. To still have that family connection."

"Most of the time." He grinned. "I suspect I'm in for a scolding, but don't worry. Her hiss is worse than her sting."

They had reached shallow water so he gathered his limbs beneath him and rose out of the sea, keeping Kate cradled in his arms.

"I can walk." She started to try and wiggle down, then stilled, probably remembering what had happened last time she tried to escape him.

"Once we are on dry land. You may find that your legs are somewhat shaky after our swim."

She sighed, but made no further attempt to climb down.

"Where have you been, Pr—" Simea began as soon as they came close.

"My apologies, Simea." From her glare, she didn't appreciate the interruption, but she let him talk. "We were caught in the storm."

"Since when has a storm on the surface ever stopped you?"

"My... slave is not used to those conditions."

"Slave? What in the Sisters is wrong with you?" Red was beginning to flare on Simea's skin. "I've never heard such nonsense. And let the poor girl down right now."

He didn't need to look to know that blue was creeping over his own skin. "I will explain everything later. Later," he repeated firmly when she opened her mouth again. "In the meantime, we are both hungry. I will take Kate to my quarters so she can refresh herself, and then I'll meet you in the kitchen."

Simea glared, then harrumphed and marched off. He was going to have to do some fast talking to calm her down.

"Wow. She's kind of scary," Kate murmured.

"Sometimes. She never let me get away with anything when I was a child." Becoming an adult hadn't made that much difference either. But she was part of his life and he adored her.

"We're on land now. You can let me down." Kate poked his chest, and he had the oddest impulse to capture that errant digit and lift it to his mouth. Would her eyes flutter closed and that intriguing shade of pink color her skin when he tasted her flesh?

He rather suspected they would, but he reluctantly put her down instead. At least this way he could admire the way the wet cloth plastered itself to the curve of her breasts and clung to the sweet indentation between her thighs. A tempting little dip that begged for his touch. She must have seen the gold flickering across his skin because she took a hasty step backwards, then swayed.

"I warned you," he said as he extended a limb to support her.

"No one likes a know-it-all," she muttered, but she leaned into his touch.

"I cannot help it if I am always right."

"Always?"

He shrugged a shoulder, then grinned at her. "Most of the time, anyway."

She rolled her eyes, then smiled back. "I'll be sure and let you know when you're wrong."

He should have been offended. Instead, he was delighted at the thought of her watching his every action. "I am sure you will. This way."

She didn't object when he tightened his limb around her and drew her against his side as he led the way to his quarters, and that was enough. For now.

CHAPTER NINE

As she leaned against A'tai and let him guide her into the house, Kate decided that this seduction business was all rather confusing. She wasn't entirely sure who was seducing whom. He certainly seemed to respond to her, but her own body responded just as quickly when he touched her. That moment in the sea when he had clasped her hands and legs, holding her helpless in his grasp, had been a revelation. She had never thought she would be the type of woman to enjoy any type of bondage, let alone from an alien octopus man. But there was no denying the rush of arousal that had swept through her in that moment. For once, her busy brain had slowed, floating in a contented haze.

She shivered at the memory, her nipples painfully hard beneath the damp cloth, and he looked down at her immediately. "Are you cold?"

Why did his obvious concern make her melt? *He's just protecting his property,* she told herself, but she didn't believe her own words.

"I'm not cold," she assured him. The warmth of the two

suns ensured an almost tropical climate, very similar to where she lived. She suspected that under other circumstances she might have found it too hot, but the constant breeze from the water created a pleasant coolness on her damp skin.

"These are our—my—quarters."

He threw open two wide glass doors to reveal a spacious room that could come from a luxury resort. The walls and floor were predominantly white, except for a tile mosaic in the center of the room, but it bore little resemblance to the sterile white of the slave ship. Colorful cushions relieved the white, and the room was filled with sunlight.

On one side, an enormous bed covered in white linens was directly across from more tall glass doors. Those doors led out onto a sheltered lanai with the sea only a few steps beyond. A comfortable seating area and a table large enough to seat at least six people occupied the rest of the spacious room.

She wandered over to the doors leading to the lanai and saw flowering vines had been trained around the posts, framing the view and filling the air with a sweet fragrance.

"This is beautiful."

"Do you think so?" A'tai frowned as he looked around the room. "The furniture is quite old. Most of it is hand-me-downs from the pal—from other places. If you would prefer something more up to date, I would be happy to provide it for you."

He thought this beautiful, luxurious room was outdated? Once again, she suspected there were a number of things he wasn't telling her, starting with his own background. Based on his attitude, she suspected he was not only wealthy, but powerful enough to expect people to obey him instantly. Given his flashes of arrogance, that didn't entirely surprise her, but it didn't explain why he was being so accommodating towards her.

He's just trying to get in your pants, a cynical voice insisted, but somehow she didn't believe it.

"The room is beautiful," she repeated. "And the furniture looks very comfortable."

"You're sure?" He still looked dissatisfied.

"Absolutely. Is there a bathroom?" she added before he could suggest any other improvements.

"Yes, of course. Although it too is not new."

She wasn't surprised when he led her through an arched passage next to the bed and into a huge, beautiful bathroom. The room contained a big bathtub in front of another window open to the view of the sea, along with the other necessities. In addition, it opened into a small enclosed courtyard with a lounging pool in the center. The courtyard walls were covered with more flowering plants, and water trickled down the rocks and into the pool.

"It is still in relatively good shape," he decided. "But if there is anything you would wish to change—"

"A'tai, stop. This is perfect. Why do you think I would want to change anything?"

"My mother likes to change things. Frequently."

"But she doesn't come here?"

He shuddered. "No, thank the Sisters. I inherited this property directly from my father. She finds it much too primitive."

Well that explained a lot.

"I'm not your mother, and I love it. Do I have time to take a bath?"

He frowned and tilted his head. "Why do you ask?"

"Because you asked Simea to make us a meal. I wouldn't want to keep her waiting."

For a second she thought he was going to dismiss her concerns despite his obvious affection for the older female, but instead he smiled.

"Trust me, she would have no hesitation in coming to get you if she was ready to serve."

She couldn't help laughing. Her brief impression of his old nurse made his statement very believable. Tall and somewhat stocky, Simea's skin was lighter than A'tai's and more heavily patterned. She had been dressed in a practical-looking navy gown that fell smoothly from her shoulders to the top of her thighs. Although she was obviously female, her chest was almost flat and there was no obvious curve to her waist or her hips. No wonder A'tai seemed so fascinated with her own body. Did he find it as strange as she found his? And as attractive?

Driven both by curiosity and her seduction plan, she ran a casual hand across her breast. His eyes immediately focused there, and she saw a quick shimmer of gold.

"Do your females have breasts like mine?" she asked as casually as she could, hoping her cheeks weren't burning.

"Not like yours." His voice sounded strained. "Although they do increase in size once they give birth and are suckling their young."

Her brain was immediately diverted. "Your females don't lay eggs?"

He finally dragged his eyes away from her breasts and looked at her, frowning. "Eggs? Why would they lay eggs?"

"That is how most of the ocean creatures in my world give birth."

"Your world?" He took a step closer, and her heart sank as she realized he was about to question her.

Before he could begin, there was the distant chime of a bell.

"That is to alert us that the meal will be ready in half an hour. If you wish to bathe, then you should do so now."

Phew. Talk about being saved by the bell. She still wasn't quite sure what she should tell him about her situation.

"Yes, that would be lovely. Do you think my dress will be dry by then?"

He looked horrified. "You cannot wear that to our meal."

"I don't exactly have anything else."

"I will find something for you," he promised. "Although it may not be completely satisfactory."

Given his notions of what was satisfactory, she wouldn't be surprised if he returned with cloth spun from gold, but she only nodded.

"I'm sure whatever you find will be just fine."

"I'll do the best I can."

He showed her how to operate the taps, and the location of an amazing array of bath products, then turned to leave. She was already testing bath salts when he stopped and returned to her side.

"Do your people have a leaving ritual?"

"You mean like a goodbye kiss? Or waving goodbye?"

"A kiss," he said firmly, then seemed to swoop towards her, lifting her into his arms.

His mouth pressed against hers, and she parted her lips. His tongue swept into her mouth, curling around hers and sucking on it with a gentle, persistent pressure that sent little streaks of excitement through her body. She no longer required his oxygen to breathe, but she clung to him as if she did.

Her arousal flared with astonishing speed. A sucking kiss to her nipple sent a spark of electricity straight to her swollen clit, and it took a moment for her to realize that one of his limbs must have curled around her breast. The reminder of their differences shocked her out of her sensual haze and she pushed back.

He lifted his head immediately, although his skin shimmered gold.

"Bath," she reminded him.

"Yes, bath." He looked as dazed as she felt, and his sucker was still working on her nipple.

"You have to let go of me," she said, resisting the urge to rub herself against his muscled abdomen.

"Yes." But he held her for another moment before his tentacle finally detached and he placed her back on the ground. "Bath. Clothes. Meal."

"Exactly."

A smile suddenly crossed his face. "I named you correctly, amali. You are very deadly."

Once again he turned to leave, and this time he didn't come back.

She climbed into the tub and settled back into the warm fragrant water with a sigh of pleasure. Her body still throbbed, and she still wasn't sure who had the upper hand in the seduction game, but she felt surprisingly triumphant. Perhaps all she needed, all these years, was an octopus man.

CHAPTER TEN

A'tai strode towards the kitchen feeling remarkably triumphant, even though his moa throbbed incessantly. Kate wanted him; he was sure of it. He only needed patience, and time to explore that luscious body. To figure out the best ways to make her sigh with pleasure and cling to him.

His triumph faded as he entered the kitchen. The wide doors of the comfortable room were open to the breeze. The carved coral table in the center had been there as long as he could remember, and the sight of Simea bending over the stove was equally familiar. Unfortunately, Simea was not giving him her usual beaming smile. Instead, she glared at him even more fiercely than she had on the beach.

"What in the Sisters are you doing, boy?"

He suddenly felt as if he were eight years old and she had just discovered him stealing a carna fruit from his mother's private garden. *I am an adult*, he reminded himself and gave her his most regal stare.

"I need clothes for Kate."

Simea didn't flinch. "Why? She's already wearing a slave gown."

Why did that reminder make him so uncomfortable?

"I don't care. I prefer her in more suitable attire."

"Suitable for what? I don't suppose you intend to put her to work scrubbing the floors. Or working in the algae farms. And if all you want is a bed companion, she doesn't need clothes for that."

"Simea, do I need to remind you that I am Prince of this House? She is to be clothed as suits my companion." Then he remembered his decision not to reveal his position. "But don't call me Prince while we are here."

She simply stared at him, tapping her fingers on the table. Her silence was as effective now as it had been when he was a child and finally, he sighed.

"What do you want to know?"

"First of all, why is she here and why are you calling her a slave? Our House has never kept slaves."

"I know. I found her on the way here. Her owner had abandoned her in a faulty escape pod and she was on the verge of drowning."

"So you rescued her." It wasn't a question, and Simea shook her head as she bent over to inspect one of her cooking pots. "You are so like your father."

Somehow, that didn't sound like a compliment. He glared at her. "What would you have done? Left her there?"

"Of course not. But neither would I be getting my limbs in a knot to look after her."

"I'm simply trying to protect her. By claiming ownership, her former master—" how he hated the sound of those words "—cannot take her back."

"The Sisters know I don't approve of slavery, but are you sure about that?"

"Under Imperial law, a slave may be removed from an unsafe situation."

"And turned into a prince's companion?"

"Why not? I would rather have her at my side than some simpering idiot my mother picks out."

Simea shot him a glance. "I see. Her ladyship has decided it's time for you to mate."

"I'm afraid so."

"And you came here rather than listen to her complaints."

Put like that, it made him sound disturbingly immature. "No. Well, yes. I know we will have to discuss it again, but I just wanted some time. And Pulata did ask me to come and inspect the forms."

"I know he's worried." Simea stirred the contents of her pot thoughtfully, momentarily diverted. "Toaga is worried too. You know we only have a small farm, but he thinks it's beginning to spread to us as well."

"Pulata said it was only about five percent."

"That matters a lot on a small farm."

"You know that I will always take care of you."

"I know." Her hand patted his shoulder as she crossed to the other side of the kitchen, and he knew he was forgiven. "But Toaga likes to make his own way. Which you should understand."

He smiled a little ruefully. Simea had certainly listened to him complain about his responsibilities often enough.

"Here." Simea put a plate of his favorite treats in front of him. He suspected she must have made them as soon as she heard he was coming. "You are too thin. Eat these while I see what I can find for your... companion."

"Thank you, Simea," he said meekly, and she laughed as she headed for the door.

"You were always much more polite once you got your way."

He had just popped the first treat in his mouth, when Toaga entered from the direction of the farms. A small, taciturn male, he was the complete opposite of his formidable spouse, but A'tai had no doubt that he was completely committed to her. He was also the only person A'tai had ever seen silence Simea with no more than a quick shake of his head.

"Prince A'tai," Toaga said, bowing his head.

"Just A'tai, please. I have a... guest, and she doesn't know that I'm a prince."

Even though he knew that Toaga would never harm Kate, he felt curiously reluctant to call her a slave to the other male. Although, Simea would undoubtedly tell him.

"So I heard."

Or had already told him, he thought ruefully as Toaga headed for the sink to wash up.

"It's not what it sounds like."

"None of my business. Of course, I doubt my female feels the same way."

He laughed. "Don't worry. She has already lectured me."

"And forgiven you, I see." Toaga gestured at the plate of treats. "What is my business is the farm. Did Pulata speak to you while he was in town?"

"Yes, he did. It's one of the reasons I'm here—to see for myself."

Toaga nodded. "I'll take you down after we eat. Your lady too, if she wants to come."

"I'm sure she won't—" He came to a sudden halt. His mother had never been interested in the farms, other than as a source of income, but he had already discovered that Kate was nothing like his mother. Remembering her curiosity, he decided that she probably would enjoy the trip. "Thank you. I think she would like that."

Simea returned with an armful of clothing. As she passed Toaga, two of their limbs entwined. It was just the briefest touch, but he found himself envying the closeness between them, the closeness of a long and patient love.

"This is all I have here in the house," Simea told him. "I can send to the palace for more."

And arouse his mother's curiosity if word got back to her—which it inevitably would. "No thank you. I'll start with these. If there's nothing suitable, I will make other arrangements."

Faiofu was the best dressmaker in the capital, he thought, already considering the possibilities, but she wasn't known for her discretion. If A'tai paid her enough, could he trust her to keep her mouth shut?

"Better get going," Toaga reminded him. "You know how long it takes females to pick out an outfit. And I'm ready for my meal."

Simea cuffed her mate affectionately. "And you'll keep waiting. I suspect that A'tai's female has been through a lot. Don't rush her, A'tai."

He suspected she was talking about far more than the clothing, but he nodded. "I won't."

As he walked back to their quarters, he sorted through the outfits. Two of them he discarded immediately—they were practical work garments like Simea habitually wore. Another one was woven from a sheer pink cloth, and as much as he would love to see her wearing it, it would do nothing to conceal her delightful body from others. He regretfully added that to the rejected pile.

The remaining two options were acceptable. One was a full-length lounging gown similar to what his mother usually wore—it wouldn't surprise him if it was one that she had discarded, probably without ever wearing. The other was a shorter day gown in a soft shade of green. He would have preferred a finer fabric, but it was well made and the color would flatter her.

Was she still in the bath, he wondered as he opened the door. The thought of her wet, naked body had him increasing his pace as he headed for the bathing room.

To his disappointment, she was no longer in the tub. Instead, she was wrapped in one of the large towels and trying to wrestle a comb through her hair. She gave him a rueful look as he entered.

"I don't think this is designed to work in my kind of hair."

"I agree. Yours is far too soft and silky." He ran his fingers through the long strands, the rich color of the precious earth that was so hard to find on Mafana. She shivered and leaned into his hand as he repeated the gesture. "Do you enjoy that?"

"Mmm. When I was little, my mother would play with my hair like that. Before she died."

"I'm sorry for your loss."

"I was very small when she died. I don't have many memories of her, but they're all happy ones." Her sea green eyes met his in the mirror. "Do you remember your father?"

"Yes. He didn't die until I became an adult. I was at the Imperial court—" On a ceremonial visit, but he didn't want to explain that to her. "On... business. He was taken ill very rapidly. I didn't even make it back in time to say goodbye."

He'd returned to find his mother distraught and bedridden and the House in complete disarray. His father had never anticipated dying at such an early age, and he had made few plans for his succession. A'tai had intended to continue his education, but instead, it had taken him the better part of the next ten years to get to the point where everything was running smoothly again, and he finally had time for his studies. And less than two years later, his mother had decided it was time for him to acquire a mate. Hadn't he sacrificed enough for his House?

Kate was still looking at him in the mirror, her eyes sympathetic, and he couldn't imagine another female in her place. All he wanted was her, and for once, he didn't care about his obligations. He couldn't ignore them forever, but for right now he was going to think only of her.

Pushing aside the thought of that unpleasant future, he made himself smile. "I brought you some clothes."

"Real clothes? Ones that actually cover my body?"

"I'm afraid so." He gave an exaggerated sigh, and she laughed. "I thought perhaps this one..."

He handed her the pale green gown he had decided was most appropriate. She stroked her hand over the fabric, but she looked a little uncertain. Damn. He knew the fabric wasn't fine enough. He quickly took it away and handed her the lounging gown instead, surprised when she still looked uncertain.

"This is not to your liking either? I will arrange for other clothing, but it will take time."

"Oh, it's very pretty," she said quickly. "Both of them are. They just don't seem very... practical."

"Why do they need to be practical?" Her objection confused him.

"It's not as if I'm just going to be lounging around all day..." Her breath caught, and he saw the uncertainty wash across her face. "Am I?"

She spun around to face him. "You don't want that, do you? I've always worked. It was bad enough on the—" She stopped, giving him a pleading look. "It would drive me crazy not to have anything to do but wait on you."

He had simply assumed that she would be available to him, but he recognized the truth in her words. Many of the females in his class worked. Even his mother's days were filled with activity.

"What type of work did you do?" he asked.

Her gaze dropped, and she peeped at him uncertainly from under her lashes. "I worked in a lab that studied ocean water."

A lab assistant? An unusual position for a slave perhaps, but now her knowledge made more sense. Not that he would permit her to take an assignment in the farm labs, but perhaps he could find something else. In the meantime, he was glad that Toaga had suggested that she accompany him.

"I have made arrangements for us to visit the algae farms this afternoon," he said, changing the subject.

Her eyes immediately sparkled with excitement. "Really? We were experimenting with them, but only on a small scale. How are you using the algae? What are you using as nutrients?"

He held up her hand, smiling at her enthusiasm, as he heard the second bell.

"I will answer all of your questions, but we don't want to be late. You still need to get dressed."

She frowned at the dresses he had offered her. "Neither of these really seems appropriate. Not that I want to be ungrateful, but couldn't you find anything else?"

He sighed and offered her the two work garments, somehow not surprised when she gave him a genuine smile.

"These are much better. If you'll just turn around for a minute, I'll get dressed."

Amused at her presumption, he obeyed. A decision made easier by the fact that he could still see her quite clearly in the mirror. She let the towel drop, revealing a far too brief glimpse of her enticing body, before she pulled the simple garment over her head.

"Okay, you can turn back around."

He had expected to be disappointed by the utilitarian garment. Instead, the deep blue color set off the creamy paleness of her skin. Because she was built so differently from a Mafanan female, her breasts strained at the material and the tight fit showed off her curves. It was almost as tempting as the slave gown, but at least it was not transparent.

"It's a little short," she said nervously.

The hem fluttered across the top of her thighs. The gown was designed not to impede the transition from the land form to the sea form, but in her case, it simply made him realize how easy it would be to slip a limb beneath the short garment.

"I do not find that a negative factor."

Pink washed her cheeks, then to his surprise, she lifted up on her toes and pressed her lips against his cheek.

"Why did you do that?"

"To thank you for listening to me."

Although he was still disappointed that she had not chosen one of the more elaborate gowns, her gratitude pleased him. As he put his arm around her and led her out of the room, he wondered what else he could do to earn her thanks.

CHAPTER ELEVEN

Before they left the suite, A'tai disappeared through a doorway Kate hadn't noticed before. He returned wearing a long, sleeveless robe. It was open down the front except for an elaborate gold pin that held it together across his pectoral muscles.

She realized it was the first time she had seen him dressed, and somehow he looked much larger and more imposing. But then she noticed that he'd chosen a dark blue color that almost exactly matched her own dress and her heart did an odd little skip.

"You look very nice," she murmured.

"Thank you, although I was hoping you would prefer me unclothed." He gave her an undeniably seductive look, then smiled when her mouth dropped open. "Come, amali. Simea said she would wait for you, but if her meal is ruined she will be unhappy."

He tugged her against him as they left the room, and she could feel the heavy silk of his robe against her side. She had no doubt that the material was expensive, but she found she actually missed the feel of his skin against hers. She'd never really thought about the fact that he was essentially naked the entire time that they were together. She supposed that without any external genitalia, there was no real need for clothing, especially in such a temperate climate. But the thought of his genitalia made her curious.

He didn't have any obvious bulges, unlike a human man, but he seemed pretty intent on exploring their physical relationship. Just where did he keep his cock? She tried to remember if she knew anything about octopus mating habits, but the only thing she could remember was a meme about detachable penises. She gave him a speculative glance just as he looked down.

"Oh no," he murmured.

"What do you mean?"

"I recognize that look. Your curiosity has been aroused. What do you want to ask?"

Hmm. Her cheeks burned, but she asked anyway. "Is your penis detachable?"

He stumbled to a halt. It was the first time she had ever seen him be anything other than graceful as he turned to stare at her in horror.

"Is that how your species mates?"

"No of course not, but—"

"Then why would you assume a Mafanan would mate in that way?"

She shifted her feet uncomfortably. "I was just trying to remember octopus biology."

With a suddenness that made her gasp, he lifted her against the wall and leaned his body against hers. One of his limbs came up to capture her wrists as he pushed himself between her legs.

"I am not a lower life form," he growled. "I assure you that my mating arm is very much attached, and I have no intention of removing it."

I shouldn't be aroused. I shouldn't be aroused. But despite her attempt to convince herself, she had never been more turned on. She wiggled experimentally against his grip, and felt him grasp her legs, locking her even more firmly in place. A slow, demanding ache started deep in her core.

"Would you like me to prove it to you, amali?" He was still growling, but his voice had dropped, vibrating through her body. She could see the gold beginning to sweep across his skin. Her mouth had gone dry, and she licked her lips nervously, half-tempted to say yes.

"Here?" Her voice came out in a nervous squeak, and his eyes darkened, but then her question seemed to penetrate and he gave a frustrated glance around. They had been passing down a long hallway and one side was completely open to the grounds.

He sighed. "I suppose not. But we will revisit this later."

"Okay," she agreed breathlessly.

His skin was still flushed gold, his eyes dark as he focused on her mouth. She waited expectantly for him to kiss her, but instead he stepped back and lowered her carefully to the ground.

"Deadly," he muttered, pulling her back against his side.

They completed the rest of their walk in silence, but her body still hummed with excitement. She could hardly wait until later. *If nothing else, I owe it to the interests of science*, she told herself with a hidden smile.

A'tai escorted her to a covered patio outside of what was obviously a kitchen. Simea raised a brow as they appeared, but Kate was glad to see that she was no longer scowling.

"You did say to take our time," A'tai reminded his nurse

"I just hope the meal is not completely ruined," Simea sniffed.

"Since you prepared it, I have no doubt at all that it will be delicious."

Simea sniffed again, but Kate saw her smile as she entered the kitchen. A'tai really could be very charming, and she could see the affection between them.

"This is Toaga," A'tai continued. "He is Simea's mate and manages the farm. Toaga, this is my... Kate."

Like Simea, Toaga's skin was lighter and more heavily patterned, and she decided it must indicate age. He also didn't have any hair, and she wondered if that too was a sign of age. Would A'tai lose his when he grew older? He would still be just as handsome, she thought as she studied his features. Not that she intended to be around to see that transition. That thought was surprisingly distressing, and it took her a moment to realize that Toaga was talking to her.

"I'm so sorry. What did you say?"

He looked from her to A'tai, and she saw the amusement on his face. God, was she really that obvious? Fortunately he didn't comment.

"I was merely welcoming you. I understand that you are looking forward to your visit to the farm."

"Yes, very much so. Are your beds on land, or floating in the sea?"

"On land? That's not a method I've heard about before."

"My understanding is that it allows for more controlled production, but it does require more land."

"That might explain it. Land is something that is in short supply around here," Toaga said. "But it is an interesting idea—"

"No more work talk at the table." Simea set a huge pot

down on the table with a bang. "You know the rules. I won't let you talk the poor girl's ears off discussing the farm."

"I really don't—" she began.

Toaga shook his head at her, his eyes warm with hidden laughter. "We can discuss it further at the farm. This looks delicious, my dear."

"I just hope it's not entirely ruined," Simea muttered as she returned to the kitchen. She brought out three more dishes before she finally sat down and joined them. "Will you offer thanks, A'tai?"

He nodded. "We thank the Sisters for the bounty of the sea and the shelter of the land, and the company of our friends and family."

"Nice to see you haven't completely forgotten what I taught you." Simea smiled at him as she began filling their plates.

"I wouldn't dare."

Simea rolled her eyes as she handed Kate an overflowing plate.

"This looks delicious," she said sincerely. Unfortunately, it also didn't look familiar.

"It is bastra, a type of seafood stew, common to the south." A'tai leaned over to explain. "The grains are from our northern territories, while the fruit is grown here on the island."

Territories? Her suspicions as to his status continued to increase, but she didn't comment. Instead, she took a cautious bite of the stew, then smiled.

"This is really good. And spicy," she added as the heat reached the back of her tongue.

Toaga laughed and handed her a glass of what turned out to be some type of iced wine. He winked at Simea. "My mate likes to heat things up."

To Kate's surprise, a flicker of blue washed over Simea's skin.

"Don't be an old fool. Now, A'tai, tell us all the gossip from the capital."

"It's not exactly my specialty," A'tai said dryly. "Although, my mother mentioned that House Faleta is opening a brothel."

Simea shook her head. "What in the Sisters is happening to this planet?"

The meal passed very pleasantly. The conversation remained general, although Kate could tell that Simea was dying to ask her questions. She drank more of the wine than she probably should have in an attempt to combat the heat of the stew, and by the time they were finished, a pleasant warmth flowed through her veins.

"Are you tired, my amali?" A'tai whispered to her as Simea brought out small cups of a bitter brew that was most definitely not coffee.

"No, why?"

He simply looked amused, and she realized she was leaning heavily against him. The combination of the midday heat, a full stomach, and the wine had made her sleepy and content.

"Oops. Sorry." She started to push herself upright, but he kept his arm wrapped around her waist. One of his limbs had crept up over her thigh as well.

"No need to apologize. I have no objection to supporting you."

Her breath caught at the look in his eyes, and for a moment she thought he was going to kiss her. Then a discreet cough sounded from across the table.

"We could postpone our trip to the farm if you wish to... rest," Toaga said.

Her cheeks heated, and she made another attempt to sit up.

This time A'tai let her go, although his arm remained around her waist. Simea watched them, a strange expression on her face.

"I'd really like to see it, if you don't mind taking us," Kate said eagerly.

"Not at all. Sire?" Toaga asked, looking at A'tai.

Sire? She felt A'tai tense, but before she could question him, Simea rose to her feet and began gathering dishes in a noisy rush. Toaga had turned blue, and it was as much for his benefit that she decided not to pursue the matter right now.

"You're still going to take me, aren't you?" she asked A'tai.

"If that is what you wish."

Did he look relieved? She turned back to Toaga. "You said that the farm was at sea. Does that mean we have to swim?"

He definitely looked relieved as he shook his head. "I had planned to take the boat."

As they all rose from the table, Simea reappeared and handed Kate a small bottle.

"This is manoji oil. To protect you from the sun."

"Thank you. And thank you for the delicious meal."

"You're most welcome." The nurse shot a quick glance at A'tai. "Very welcome indeed."

Kate wasn't sure exactly how to take her words, so she only smiled and went to join Toaga and A'tai, who were waiting at the dock on one side of the wide beach. As she approached, she could see the small boat had two outriggers and a colorful sail.

A'tai looked chagrined as she joined them. "I should have thought of the oil. Your skin is so delicate. Do you need help applying it?"

He took a step towards her, and she hastily backed away. The thought of him rubbing oil into her skin was a little too appealing, and she was determined to see the algae farm.

"I can do it, thank you."

But even though only her hands applied the oil, his eyes followed her so closely that it almost felt as if he had been doing it. By the time she finished, her cheeks were flushed and her body hummed with arousal. Doing her best to ignore the sensation, she went to join him at the boat.

CHAPTER TWELVE

As A'tai helped Kate into the boat, he could feel the slickness of the manoji oil on her skin. It was a disturbingly erotic sensation, and he found himself wondering if her tight little cunt would be as slippery. His arousal had been simmering since he'd had her pressed against the wall earlier, and he almost regretted ever suggesting the trip to her.

But as she leaned forward to ask Toaga a question, her eyes sparkling, he didn't have the heart to suggest canceling it. She had agreed to let him show her how their bodies could fit together later, and he would just have to wait until then.

He didn't contribute to the conversation, content just to watch her. As the boat skimmed across the water, the Sisters' rays struck sparks of gold in the rich brown of her hair. Her pale skin shimmered softly from the oil. He wondered how she would look if he stripped her naked and applied it to the rest of her body—and this time, he would most definitely be the one doing the application.

As they rounded the headland into the first bay, she looked back at him and her eyes widened. He realized that his lustful thoughts were reflected in the gold flickering across his skin. He took a deep breath to try and compose himself, but her sweetness was heavy in the air and it wasn't until he saw Pulata waiting for them, that he managed to focus on business once more.

Pulata was dressed in the standard working male's tunic, but it was the same deep blue as Kate's dress, and for some reason he found that annoying. He also didn't like the speculative way that Pulata looked at Kate.

He helped her out of the boat, then stood with his arm around her.

"Kate, this is Warden Pulata. He oversees the management of the algae farms. Pulata, this is my Kate."

"Greetings, Lady Kate and Pr—A'tai." Pulata shot a quick look at Toaga, and A'tai realized the older male must have alerted him that he preferred not to use his title. He should have thought to warn the Warden himself. He was actually surprised that Kate had not already followed up on Toaga's earlier slip up. He had already noticed how observant she was —which she immediately proved as she turned to survey the farms.

The algae beds were arranged in neat formation across the surface of the bay, with colored buoys indicating the ownership of each bed. The space between the beds was filled with floating docks to enable the farmers to work on them more easily.

"What do the colors of the buoys represent? Are they different types of algae, or are they under different ownership?"

"The top color represents the owner while the bottom color represents the species," Pulata answered before A'tai could respond.

"It looks as if the majority of them belong to one owner."

"That is correct. This island is one of the primary production centers for Prince A—I mean, for House Maulimu." Pulata shot him a nervous look, but Kate seemed more interested in the actual farm.

She surveyed the beds thoughtfully. "It looks as though certain species grow better in certain parts of the bay."

Pulata bowed his head. "You are correct. The far side receives afternoon shade and is better suited for growing the species which are used for fuel."

"Are you extracting their oil or compressing them into pellets for fuel use?"

Pulata's expression turned from speculative to impressed. Kate moved to his side, and he turned to point out the processing mill on the far shore. A'tai scowled after them while Toaga gave him a sympathetic look.

"Your... companion is full of questions."

"Yes, she is." He had enjoyed it when she was asking him questions—he was not quite so sure that he appreciated her intense interest in another male's conversation.

His annoyance continued to grow as Pulata shepherded them through the tour of the beds. Kate continued to ask questions—questions which revealed a surprising amount of knowledge—and he could see Pulata falling under her spell. By the time they reached one of the beds that had suffered damage, his patience was wearing thin.

"This is one of the beds that I was telling you about, A'tai," Pulata said, and A'tai almost snapped at him to use his correct title before he came to his senses.

The bed was in terrible condition, dark viscous streaks beginning to overtake the healthy yellow. It was only one bed amongst many, but seeing it in person, he could understand Pulata's concern, especially if it was spreading.

"Have you tried isolating the affected beds?"

"Of course. But it seems to spring up at random with no

relation between the beds that are affected and the ones that are not."

"Once it starts, is there any way to rescue the remaining algae?" Kate asked.

Pulata shook his head. "We tried removing the unaffected portions but none of them survived."

"It's possible that they were already infected at a microscopic level," she said thoughtfully.

"That was my conclusion as well." Pulata pointed to a distant boat that was traveling slowly between the beds. "We are collecting samples from every bed on a weekly basis. But none of the samples has shown any sign of the disease, even when taken from beds that are later infected."

"That's interesting. It suggests that it's environmental." Kate turned to survey the beds again. "But there is no pattern as to where it appears?"

"Not that we have been able to determine."

"But there were more empty beds on the sunny side of the bay. Is that due to position, or the type of algae?"

Pulata frowned. "I'm not sure if we correlated those parameters. Would you like to accompany me to the lab?"

The question was addressed specifically to Kate, and A'tai's irritation flared again. He stepped up and put his arm around her shoulders.

"I don't think we have time—"

"Please, A'tai," Kate interrupted. "I'd really like to see the lab."

How could he refuse her when she looked up at him hopefully?

"Very well," he conceded, trying not to sound annoyed.

"This way." Pulata led the way along the floating dock and to A'tai's annoyance, Kate slipped free from his arm and went to join the warden.

"I have some work to do on my bed," Toaga said quietly. "With your permission?"

"Yes, yes," he muttered impatiently, as he watched Kate talking to Pulata without even a glance back in his direction.

"You know," Toaga said thoughtfully, "Lady Kate reminds me of you."

"Of me?"

"You act the same way when you are deep in your studies. I suspect you've made a good choice in your… companion."

Toaga walked off before A'tai could respond. His initial impulse was to deny the statement, but it bore an uncomfortable ring of truth. As he hurried to catch up with Kate and Pulata, he continued to think about it. She acted more like a scholar than a slave, he decided—a theory that was confirmed when they reached the lab.

She was obviously familiar with the majority of the equipment, which would be expected if she had been an assistant, but she was also clearly familiar with the protocols around setting up and analyzing experiments.

"That's an interesting hypothesis," Pulata said. "Perhaps it would be possible for you to come and work on it here with me? We have an opening."

A'tai had been so busy speculating about the delightful puzzle that Kate represented that he had not been paying much attention, but those words penetrated. Let his female come and work in a subservient position with another male?

"Absolutely not," he roared.

They both looked startled, then Kate came over and put a soothing hand on his arm.

"Please, A'tai. I'd really like to help discover what is happening to the algae. Pulata says it's vital to the economy of the people who employ him. They own most of the beds in the bay."

This time, he was not about to be swayed by her pleading eyes. She belonged to him, not to Pulata.

"No."

"Why not? I know I can help."

"I said no." Her insistence only made him more determined. He didn't like the fact that she seemed so comfortable here in Pulata's company, and he was not going to allow her to spend any more time with him.

"But—"

"I said no," he repeated, and made a fatal mistake. "You are my slave, and you will obey me."

Shock washed over her face, followed by a heart-wrenching combination of anger and despair. She stumbled away from him, then turned and raced for the door.

Fuck. How could he have been such an idiot?

As he started to go after her, Pulata stepped in front of him, his face stern and angry.

"Is this true, sire? She is your slave?"

"No! Well, yes, but it is not what you think."

"I think you just treated an obviously intelligent, thoughtful person as if they were no more than an insect beneath your feet."

Fury roared through A'tai, and he extended his limbs, towering over the shorter male.

"This is not your business. She belongs to me."

Pulata stood his ground. "As a slave? Or as a companion?"

The question penetrated his anger.

"I am not questioning the tie between you," Pulata added softly. "But I think you had best consider the nature of that tie before you lose her."

He couldn't quite bring himself to admit the other male was right, but he relaxed his posture.

"I will talk to her."

Pulata wisely stepped aside without further comment, and A'tai went after his female. But when he stepped outside, she was nowhere in sight.

He scanned the area frantically, searching for any sign of her. At this hour of the day, many of the workers took a break to avoid the full heat of the sun and the area was practically deserted. He wondered if she had gone to find Toaga, but he could see the older male in the distance, bending over his beds.

Where in the Sisters had she gone?

He was about to dive into the water to search for her, when he realized he was being foolish. She was of the land, not of the sea. She would not have taken to the water to escape.

His heart pounded as he turned to look at the densely wooded slope leading up from the bay. The jungle contained so many dangers, and she would be facing them alone. She was so fragile. *If anything happens to her, I will never forgive myself,* he thought as he headed for the trees.

CHAPTER THIRTEEN

Kate raced out of the lab, doing her best not to give in to the tears that threatened. After their original conversation, it had been surprisingly easy to forget that A'tai thought of her as no more than a slave. He had never treated her that way —until just now.

She burst out into the sunlight, a little surprised she had made it that far without him following her. The jade waters of the bay sparkled peacefully under the brilliant rays of the two suns, the colorful algae beds adding to the vibrant scene, but it all looked horribly alien. She had to get away, but how? Where?

A bird called from behind her, and she whirled around to find herself looking up at the wooded slope that led into the interior of the island. It wasn't exactly like an Earth forest, but right now it seemed vastly more familiar than the waters of the bay. Without pausing to consider her decision, she headed for the trees.

The undergrowth at the base of the hill was annoyingly thick, but once she had fought her way through it, the ground beneath the trees was much clearer. The temperature also dropped under the shade of the canopy, and she gave a sigh of relief as she started to make her way up the hillside.

As she climbed, her initial urgency began to fade, and she wondered if she had been too impulsive. She had accepted A'tai's terms, intending all along to use him to gather information on how to find her friends and then escape. She had forgotten about that part of the plan in her enthusiasm over the work that they were doing at the algae farms, so closely allied to her own work back on Earth.

If nothing else, A'tai's reprehensible behavior had simply reminded her that she was alone in an alien world. Maybe it was time to discover if there were other options. The farms clearly required a large number of workers, and Simea had mentioned a village. If she could make her way there, perhaps she could find a way to reach the capital.

None of the Mafanans she had met so far had seemed to bear her any ill will, and Simea had certainly been shocked when A'tai announced that she was his slave. Maybe she could find someone equally sympathetic to help her.

But although she tried to occupy herself with plans for the future, she kept returning to thoughts of A'tai. The way he smiled at her, and the way he wanted to protect her. Was that why he had so adamantly refused to consider her working with Pulata? Did he think she would be in some kind of danger? Was there more to his arrogance than just a desire to control her?

Her chest ached, and she told herself it was due to the exertion of the climb, but she knew she was lying to herself.

When she finally reached the top of the ridge, she found herself in a shaded clearing. On one side, the ground continued to climb upwards, growing increasingly barren. A small waterfall trickled down the rocky slope. From the other side of the clearing, she could see a much larger bay. A harbor occupied one end, while a village stretched out along the remaining shoreline. White buildings lush with flowers were stacked along the water's edge. At the far end of the bay the ground rose steeply into a rocky promontory, crowned with a large white building that reminded her of a fairytale castle. It too was covered with flowers.

The hillside leading down from her position to the village was also densely wooded, but it didn't look like a difficult descent. The boats floating in the harbor promised a way off the island, if she could find one willing to take her on board. Hadn't that been her plan all along? To escape and find her friends? All she needed to do was to descend the hill, but her feet didn't want to move.

She kept thinking about A'tai. His arrogance and his unexpected sweetness. The way his touch set off fireworks in her body.

I don't want to leave him, she realized. *But how can I stay and be his slave?*

Was that really how he thought of her? As upset as she had been, she had seen the regret that flashed across his face as soon as he spoke. But was that enough? Would he bring it up again as soon as she wanted to do something of which he didn't approve?

Her mind and her heart wrestled with the decision. Still debating her options, she went to the waterfall to collect some water. The cool liquid trickled down her throat, making her realize how thirsty she had been from the climb.

As she went back to collect a second handful, the rocks seemed to move. A strange creature perched there, its body almost invisible against the rocks until it changed position. Bulbous black eyes stared at her as it raised its tail, a tail as long and thick as her leg. The scientific part of her brain noted that it bore a distinct resemblance to a scorpion, but the rest of her was paralyzed by fear as she saw the clear liquid glistening on the pointed tip of its tail.

It's going to sting me, and I'll never see A'tai again.

The thought broke through her paralysis, and she tensed, preparing to move as soon as it attacked. The tail rose higher, then darted towards her at a shocking speed. She tried to throw herself to one side, already knowing that she wouldn't make it.

And then A'tai was there. He crouched over her body, his limbs forming a protective wall around her as he seized the tail right below the glistening point. The creature made a high screeching noise, twisting around to try and attack A'tai with its claws, but he was too fast for it. Two of his limbs grabbed the claws, wrenching the creature apart and tossing the carcass aside without a second look as he turned to her.

Frantic hands searched her body. "Are you hurt? Did it sting you?"

The tears that had been pending since she left the lab suddenly burst free. She tried to reach for him, but he was inspecting her even more urgently now.

"Where's the wound? I need to stop the venom from flowing into the rest of your body."

"Not... not wounded." She managed to sob out the words, and he collapsed down next to her, pulling her into his lap.

"Thank the Sisters. I've never been so terrified. You must never run away like that again."

She only cried harder, trying to bury her face against his chest.

He tightened his arms around her, rocking her back and forth. "Please stop crying, amali. If you want to work in the lab, you can work in the lab. Just don't leave me."

"I... I wasn't leaving you."

"You weren't?"

"No," she admitted to him, and to herself. No matter how tempting the village appeared, she knew she had been about to march back down the hill and confront him. "But we need to talk."

His arms tightened at the caveat.

"What do you want to talk about?" he asked suspiciously, and she had the sudden urge to laugh. It appeared that no male ever wanted to hear his female say they needed to talk.

"You know that everything about this place is strange to me," she said slowly.

"I know. You said you had never been to Mafana before."

She took a deep breath, determined to trust him. "It's not just Mafana. It's everything—aliens, spaceships, the Empire. My world isn't aware of any of it."

Shock covered his face, rapidly replaced by understanding. "You come from a pre-spaceflight world?"

"Yes. I mean, we have spaceships, but they don't go very far." She clutched his hand. "Does that mean if the Royal Fleet finds me or my friends they'll take us away and put us in prison?"

"Of course not. Why would you think that?"

"It's what the slavers said. That we were illegal."

"It is illegal for them to steal you away from your world. It does not make you illegal. The Royal Fleet would not imprison you." He gave her an unexpectedly sympathetic look. "But neither would they return you."

"So there's no way to return to Earth," she said softly. She waited for dismay to swamp her, but all she felt was resigned acceptance. She suspected she had recognized that it was a one-way trip a long time ago.

"I am afraid not. No reputable ship would make the journey. And the less reputable ones would be no better than the slavers who took you." His face hardened. "There are many worlds where your background would make you vulnerable to being enslaved."

She choked back a sob as she thought about her friends again.

"Is that true even on Mafana?"

He sighed. "I would like to say no, but there are unscrupulous people everywhere."

"I have to find my friends. I'm worried that someone will take advantage of them."

"I understand. When we return to the house, I will have my agent start some discreet inquiries."

"Your agent?"

He gave her a rueful look. "I suppose since we are revealing all our secrets, there is something you should know about me."

"You mean the fact that you're Prince A'tai of House Maulimu?"

She wasn't sure exactly when she had reached the conclusion, but the various hints had been coming together in her mind. The castle in the village below had been the final piece. He looked so shocked she felt rather smug. Then he burst into laughter and hugged her.

"My amali. I should have known that you would figure it out. I will never be able to keep any secrets from you, will I?"

Her smugness disappeared in a wave of uncertainty. He spoke as if they would be together for a long time. Did he really mean it?

"So what happens now?" she asked.

"We return home."

"To your castle?"

"Not unless you insist. I was coming here to get away from that life."

"Why?"

"Because my mother is insisting—" He came to an abrupt

halt. "Insisting that I take a greater interest in the future of the House. I was more concerned with the present and the issue with the algae."

She was quite sure that he still wasn't telling her everything, but she let it drop for now, more concerned about their argument.

"Did you really mean what you said about letting me work at the lab?"

He scowled, but he looked like a pouty little boy rather than an angry Prince. "Yes, but I do not like it. You will be away from me all day."

When he put it like that, she wasn't quite as enthusiastic. So much of her life had consisted of nothing but work and sleep and study. Even the short time they had spent together had shown her that there was far more to life than that.

"Maybe it could be a part-time kind of thing," she suggested. "Do you think Pulata would allow that?"

"He works for me. He will do whatever I tell him to do."

"You're very good at ordering people around, aren't you? Do they always do what you tell them to do?"

"Perhaps we should experiment." His eyes heated. "Kiss me, my amali."

She shouldn't, she really shouldn't, but Lord, did she want to.

"Please," he added, and that decided it. She obeyed.

CHAPTER FOURTEEN

Kate put her hand on A'tai's neck, trying to tug his mouth down to hers. Instead, two of his limbs curled beneath her butt, lifting her easily until their faces were at the same height. He looked at her with glowing golden eyes, but he didn't move. She leaned forward and brushed her lips across his, slowly, teasingly, half-expecting him to take over. Instead, he remained absolutely still as she ran her tongue along the seam of his mouth, reveling in his clean, salty taste. But then she bit down gently on his lower lip, and he roared.

Somehow she ended up on her back with him leaning over her, kissing her hungrily as he took control. She returned the kiss just as eagerly, her arms clasping his neck and her legs coming up to circle his waist. As he explored her mouth she felt two of his limbs curving up around her breasts, and then his suckers fastened on her nipples. Even through the cloth of her dress, the suction sent streaks of excitement straight to her needy clit.

He made an impatient sound, then ripped the front of her dress open in one quick move. The velvety mouth of his suckers closed over her nipples again, the direct contact shockingly intense. More of the small sucking kisses covered the rest of her breasts. Another limb made its way between her legs, pressing kisses to her inner thigh. She instinctively tried to pull her legs together, and a strong limb immediately closed around each leg, gently but firmly pulling them apart and opening her to his exploration. Her mind stuttered to a stop.

The thick length wound between her lower lips, sucking at the sensitive flesh. And then a sucker closed directly over her clit, and she came with a sudden, overwhelming force. She heard herself cry out, but it seemed to come from somewhere far away. Her body shuddered helplessly as A'tai stopped kissing her and raised his head to look down at her.

He seemed almost as shocked as she felt as she floated back to earth.

"What is this place on your body?"

"My clit." Her voice still sounded odd in her ears.

"Human males are very lucky to have such an easy way to pleasure their females."

She would have laughed, but her body was still quivering.

"And it produces such a delicious result." His suckers were still moving gently between her legs, and she realized he was tasting the results of her climax.

"I wish to try this again."

Her ability to speak disappeared as the sucker over her clit began pulling again, gentler this time, rocking back and forth sensually until she slid over into a long, slow climax.

When her eyes fluttered open that time, his skin was completely gold, his eyes intent on her face.

"Do you remember our earlier conversation?"

Her heart skipped a beat, but she nodded.

"Do you still wish to learn about my mating arm?"

She didn't hesitate. She had never wanted anything more. "Yes."

He raised her arms over her head, holding her wrists together with one strong hand, while the limbs curled around her thighs pulled her legs further apart. Even her labia were spread open before she felt the press of his cock—no, his moa—at her entrance.

She tried to analyze the sensation as he pressed inside, impossibly wide and thick, but he tightened his grip as he entered and her mind stopped working. All she could do was feel. Feel the constant pull at her breasts, feel the velvety strokes against her clit, feel herself being stretched open.

He kept going, sinking deeper and deeper into her body, until he filled her completely. Her pussy quivered, little ripples of pleasure surging through her as her body tried to adjust. All these years, she had never realized what she was missing, but as she opened her eyes and saw an answering ecstasy on his face, she had no regrets.

A'TAI WATCHED AS HIS MATING ARM ENTERED KATE'S impossibly small cunt. His moa was furled as tightly as possible, and still he struggled to work his way inside the tight little channel. Her silken flesh surrounded him, impossibly hot, and so sweet that he could have sipped at her nectar for hours, but his moa was too impatient.

He drew back, then thrust forward, his passage only slightly easier this time. Then he remembered her magical pleasure button and concentrated on it. He felt her shudder, then more of her delicious essence surrounded him, her channel milking his moa in long pulsing waves. His control vanished, and he thrust again and again as his moa began to unfurl, widening as her channel grew even hotter and slicker.

His seed gathered into a hot ball at the base of his moa as he tried to resist, tried to prolong the overwhelming pleasure. But then she began to convulse around him again and restraint was impossible. His seed rushed into her in an endless wave until she had pulled the last drop from his body and he collapsed down over her, completely spent.

He released her arms and legs, and they slid limply to the ground. Her weakness concerned him but when he raised his head, she was smiling up at him.

"Wow. I never knew it would be like that."

"No male has ever pleasured you as well?" He couldn't help preening a little, even though the thought of another male touching her silken skin made his arms tighten instinctively. She was his now.

"No male has ever pleasured me at all," she said.

"Then they were unworthy, thoughtless males."

"I don't think you understand. I've never had sex before."

"Never?" How was it possible that such a desirable female had not been courted?

"Never."

"Human males are fools," he said firmly, doing his best to hide his delight. He knew that it was unworthy, but the fact that he had been the only one to enter her sweet little cunt filled him with possessive pride.

"I always thought so." She laughed, the movement making her fascinating breasts quiver gently. They were flushed pink and covered with small red circles, the symbols of his possession. Would they last, he wondered, or would he have to renew them each time.

To his shock, his moa began to swell again. He had always been told that it would subside as soon as his seed was delivered but it didn't seem to have received the message.

Her eyes widened as she felt him grow inside her, and her channel fluttered around him.

"You're hard again already?"

"It would appear so." He withdrew slightly, far enough to see his moa glistening with her nectar, the deep teal a shocking contrast to her pink flesh as she stretched open around him. It still seemed impossible that she could welcome him into her body.

"Then Mafanan females are very lucky," she murmured, her hips lifting to chase his moa.

"I'm not sure it is common," he admitted as he rewarded her by thrusting back into her channel. They both moaned.

"You mean you're special because you're a prince?" He could tell she was trying to tease him, but her voice was breathless with pleasure.

"No, I mean I have no experience. My mating arm has never been inside another female."

"Then Mafanan females are fools," she said, echoing his earlier words, but he could see the same delight on her face. "Why—"

His limbs pulled her back into the mating position as he bent his head and kissed her, stroking in and out of her in a slow, steady rhythm. When he released her mouth, her face was soft, dazed with pleasure.

"If you wish, we can discuss our respective pasts in great detail, but later." He thrust a little harder, his moa already threatening to unfurl. "Much later."

"Okay," she whispered, trying to wiggle in his grip. "Do that again."

He obliged, and there was no more discussion.

. . .

A very long time later, A'tai carried his sleeping mate back down the hill. Since he had ruined her gown, he wrapped her in his robe instead. She barely stirred. He had to remember how delicate she was, he reminded himself. Even though she accepted him into her body so eagerly and deliciously, he must take care not to wear her out.

The Sisters were beginning to set when he reached the farms, and there was a hum of activity as the farmers ended their day. He managed to avoid them, slipping quietly into the waters to make his way back along the shore to their cottage. Her eyes opened as the water rose over her body and she smiled.

"We always seem to end up in the water."

"It's part of who I am." He let his limbs propel them home, careful to keep her head above the water as he cradled her in his arms.

"Then I can't complain." Her eyes traveled past him to the brilliant colors of the sunset. "It's so beautiful here."

"A fitting setting for your beauty," he agreed.

She smiled again, even as her eyes began to close. "You're such a sweet talker."

"Rest, amali. Tomorrow is another day."

For some reason that made her laugh, but by the time he carried her into their rooms she was asleep again. She didn't move as he carefully cleansed her, then took her to bed. Even though his apparently insatiable moa throbbed eagerly at the sight of those lush, pale curves marked with the signs of his possession, he simply wrapped himself around her and let her sleep.

CHAPTER FIFTEEN

A band of sunlight found its way through a gap in the curtains and into Kate's eyes. The last thing she remembered was A'tai carrying her into the ocean. She must have slept through the entire night. Her entire body felt limp and relaxed. She tried to give a satisfied stretch and discovered that she was locked in A'tai's embrace. He hadn't changed into his land form, and his limbs were curved around and between her legs and curled around her breasts. As soon as she tried to move, his grip tightened, then relaxed. He rolled her over on her back and smiled down at her.

"Good morning, my Kate."

"Good morning. I'm sorry I fell asleep on you."

"I believe my moa is to blame." His eyes glinted with satisfaction, and she could already see the gold beginning to tint his skin.

"I suspect you're right." She gasped as a velvety sucker brushed across her nipple, triggering an immediate surge of arousal. "It does seem to be insatiable."

He bent his mouth to her neck, kissing his way down the sensitive skin. "Only because you are so delicious."

"Mmm." Her thoughts disappeared in a pleasured daze.

He reached her breasts, his mouth closing over the taut peak of her nipple, shockingly hot and wet. His tongue played with the sensitive tip, working it until it felt swollen and distended. She tried to arch against his mouth, and then he had captured her hands and was pulling her legs apart.

A distant thought penetrated the fog of pleasure.

"Wait."

He stopped immediately. "Yes, amali?"

"Do you always have to have sex like this?"

"I don't understand. It is the mating position."

"Why do you always hold my hands and legs?"

"Do you not enjoy it?"

A shiver skated over her skin as she remembered the previous day. "I enjoy it very much, but that's not what I asked."

"A female will fight if she's not restrained. She could injure herself or her mate. The mating position ensures that she will be adequately pleasured."

"Really? Your females always fight?"

"You forget, I have no experience." He tilted his head, a thoughtful expression crossing his face. "But perhaps not. I am not sure if it is driven by biology or by custom."

"I'm not going to fight you," she assured him.

"But you do not wish to mate?"

"I want to very much, but I also want to explore you. Can you let me do that?"

"If that is what you desire." Despite his agreement, she could see the tension in his body.

"I think you'll enjoy it. If you don't, just tell me to stop. Now roll over on your back."

KATE AND THE KRAKEN

For a moment she thought he'd refuse, but he eventually did as she requested. All of the gold had disappeared from his skin. She paused to admire him—his strong, muscular upper body, the thick, graceful limbs splayed across the sheets.

She let her hand wander across his broad chest, circling the small points of his nipples. As she did, she caught a hint of gold. Interesting. It appeared that his nipples were also sensitive. She bent her head and sucked one into her mouth. His body arched as he gave an audible gasp.

"Kate!"

She gave him a smug smile as she sat back on her heels. "I told you you'd like it."

"I have never... I didn't know..."

"Let's see what else you didn't know."

She teased the other nipple, then slowly kissed her way down his stomach. His limbs thrashed restlessly, but he didn't attempt to restrain her. She slid her hand carefully between them and felt a long, hard ridge with a definite bulge beneath it. He groaned as she traced the length of it.

"Am I hurting you?"

"Sisters, no."

She stroked it again, and it flowered open as his mating arm emerged. Her mouth dropped open. She wasn't quite sure what she had expected. Her memories consisted mostly of size and pressure and an amazing curling movement. But his moa was shockingly different from a human penis. A thick base covered with tiny suckers opened into a wide, flat shaft with a pointed tip. Her hand looked small in comparison. There was no way that could have fit inside her.

The surface of his moa was a deep, rich teal, glistening faintly and she touched it with a cautious finger. At her touch, he groaned again and the sides of his shaft rolled inwards to form a long thick cylinder. Ah. He was still intimidatingly large, but the shape was much more compatible with her own body.

She didn't bother to ask if she was hurting him. From the gold washing over his skin, he was most definitely not in pain. She stroked him again, and this time his moa curled around her finger in a powerful grip.

"Can you control the shape?" she asked, as she slid her finger in and out.

"To an extent." He sounded dazed, and she smiled.

"Try and keep it curled like that. I want to try something."

"What do you—oh, fuck!"

His question ended in a strangled moan as she closed her mouth over the tip of his moa. Even furled into a tight cylinder, it was too big for her to take more than an inch or two, but she did her best. She'd never dreamed she would want to do this for any man, but she wanted to please A'tai. As she felt his body tense and heard him moan with pleasure, her own excitement built to match his. She stroked her tongue down the center of the cylinder and he let out a hoarse cry.

A second later, she was on her back, her hands and legs held tightly in his grasp as he plunged into her, his seed exploding in a heated rush as her own orgasm washed over her and left her shuddering beneath him.

"I'm sorry," he murmured a short time later, after her pulse had slowed and her breathing returned to normal.

"Why are you sorry?"

"I was not supposed to take you in the mating position."

"I didn't object," she said softly. "And we can always try it again."

He shuddered and she felt him start to expand again, but she pushed gently against his chest. "Later. Right now, I have work to do."

His body stiffened, and she wondered if he would refuse to

let her go. But he pulled out of her channel without protest and went to run her a bath.

The rest of the day did not go nearly so well. Although A'tai reluctantly sent her off with Toaga, by the time she returned, he was aggressively unhappy. He snapped at everyone except her, and as soon as she had eaten, he dragged her back to their rooms to make love to her until she was a limp, quivering—and extremely satisfied—mess.

She had missed him as well, more than she had expected, so when he proposed accompanying her the following day, she didn't object. Unfortunately, that was even worse. He shadowed her every move, and growled at Pulata each time he came near her. Once again he dragged her off as soon as they returned home.

On the third day, she decided it would be better for everyone if she spent a day at the house instead. But she couldn't help worrying about the status of her experiments, and after wandering around restlessly, she went to join Simea in the kitchen, hoping to make herself useful. Instead, she found herself snapping at the older female.

"I'm so sorry," she said, as soon as she realized what she had done.

Simea shook her head. "The two of you are going to be the death of me. Go find A'tai and work this out."

Much calmer because she was staying home, he had excused himself after breakfast and gone to his study. She expected him to be working at some kind of royal business, but when she joined him, he was examining an old scroll through a magnifying lens.

"This is really quite fascinating," he said, then frowned. "I thought you were going to spend the morning with Simea."

"Yeah, that didn't work out."

"Do you need me?" His skin flickered gold, but she backed away.

"I think I need some time to recover first. You've been rather... enthusiastic for the past two days."

"Have I injured you?"

He looked so horrified that her annoyance vanished. "Not at all. But I can't spend all of my time in bed."

"I didn't intend to leave this room."

She laughed. "You know what I mean. Don't worry about me. I'm just anxious about the results of that last experiment and it's making me grumpy."

His conflicting feelings were clearly written on his face, but he said stiffly. "I could accompany you to the lab."

"I think we both know that won't end well." She sighed and wandered around the room, examining the spines of all the books she couldn't read. "All that work to get my doctorate and now I can't even read a simple children's book."

"I am not sure that word translates correctly. You are a physician?"

"No. It means I have a higher level degree. Mine is in biochemistry with a focus on marine environments."

He looked startled. "I suspected you might be a scholar, but I didn't realize the extent of your knowledge. That explains a lot."

"Why did you think I knew so much about the production of algae?" She did her best not to feel insulted, but she couldn't completely suppress her irritation.

"You said you were a lab assistant. I simply assumed your natural intelligence and curiosity had led you to learn more." He gave her a sympathetic smile. "Believe me, I understand how frustrating it is not to be able to complete your research. I have been trying to complete this paper on Namoan trade routes for three months now."

Her mouth dropped open. "You're writing a paper?"

"Now you seem surprised," he said dryly.

"I thought you were busy being a prince," she said weakly. Apparently she was just as guilty of leaping to conclusions. Even though he was clearly intelligent, she had assumed that such a vibrantly physical male wouldn't bother with intellectual pursuits.

He rubbed his neck thoughtfully. "Do you need to be at the farm to complete your work?"

"Not necessarily, but that's where the lab is located."

"Ah. If that's the only issue, then it is easily remedied." He picked up a communication device and began issuing a series of orders while she stared at him.

"Did you just tell someone to build me a lab?" she asked when he finished his call.

"Yes. Fortunately, we can repurpose one of the existing outbuildings so it will be ready by tomorrow afternoon."

"Just like that?"

"Just like that. I should have thought of it before. You will be able to continue your work, but you will still be close by."

She shook her head, then moved around the desk and seated herself on his lap. He was in land form, but one of his limbs immediately unfurled and wrapped around her leg.

"Thank you, A'tai."

"You are very welcome, my amali."

She expected him to kiss her, but instead he studied her face.

"Perhaps we should spend the time between now and tomorrow finding out what else we don't know about each other."

"I haven't led a very exciting life. I'm just an ordinary human."

"You are very far from ordinary," he said firmly. "Tell me about the place where you were born."

"A small town in the middle of nowhere. I got out of there as soon as I could and never went back. What about you?"

"I was born here on the island." His lips twisted. "Unintentionally. Apparently, I came early and my mother was unable to make it back to the palace for a full, ceremonial birth. It was the first time I disappointed her."

"I don't believe you are a disappointment."

"I suspect she would disagree," he said dryly, then shrugged. "I honestly don't know. We do not communicate well, but she is very much a part of running the House. I couldn't do it without her," he added slowly.

"Do you have any brothers or sisters?"

"No." He hesitated. "Her physician once told me she was unable to have more children, but I was never quite sure."

He shook his head as if dismissing the problem and turned back to her. "Do you have any siblings?"

"I was one of three girls. My older sister was beautiful and popular and pregnant at seventeen. She married her high school boyfriend, and the last time I saw her, she was working on baby number four." *A baby I'll never get to see,* she thought sadly. But then again, she had barely seen the other three. She dutifully sent gift cards at Christmas and on their birthdays, but she rarely visited them. It hadn't helped that she disliked Louisa's husband Paul almost as much as he disliked her. "But she seems happy enough."

"And your younger sister?"

"She died young from an incurable disease. It's one of the reasons I studied so hard. I wanted to be a doctor—until I got to pre-med and realized that I was the wrong person to be around sick people. I decided to look for other ways to make a difference."

"What about your parents?"

"My mother died when my younger sister was born. My father was a bully who thought that higher education just made people think they were better than they were. We did not get along." *And wasn't that an understatement.*

He gave her a rueful smile. "I'm not entirely sure my mother would disagree. She wanted me to have an education, of course, at the right schools, but any type of advanced degree was quite unnecessary."

"Why are our relationships with our parents so complicated?"

"I don't know. I intend to make sure my children know that they are loved."

The realization struck her with blinding suddenness. She wouldn't be able to give him children. Their species were too different to be compatible. Her chest suddenly ached. She hadn't realized until this moment how much she would have liked to have had a family with him. If he wanted to have children, he would have to choose a Mafanan female—and then what would become of her?

"Amali? Kate, is something wrong?"

"No, I was just thinking."

"That is always dangerous," he said gravely, but his beautiful golden eyes were smiling.

Didn't he realize there was no future for them?

She forced a smile, then deliberately arched her back, thrusting her breasts against the tight fabric of her gown. His eyes heated and gold flickered across his skin. She let her hand slide down between them, slipping between his limbs until she felt the hard ridge of his moa. Her fingers traced the opening of his sheath as he groaned.

"You said you needed to recover."

"I'm feeling much better."

"But we were getting to know each other," he protested weakly, but his eyes were fixed on her movements.

"And we still are. In *intimate* detail."

His sheath opened, and the heavy length of his engorged moa filled her hand. He growled, and then the papers on top of his desk went flying as he bent her across the surface.

She was right. She had completely recovered.

CHAPTER SIXTEEN

A week later, A'tai watched in satisfaction as Kate disappeared into her lab. This was a much better solution than allowing her to work at the farm lab. Although she continued to go there—and Pulata visited her here—the visits were short enough to be no more than a minor annoyance.

Their days had fallen into an easy rhythm. They spent the mornings working, then had lunch with Simea and Toaga. The afternoons were spent together, talking and discovering each other. He had told her more about himself than he had ever revealed to anyone. She seemed to be equally as transparent, and yet he had the feeling that something was bothering her.

His satisfaction faded as he considered the problem. Was it because they had still not received any word of her friends? His agent was searching—and had offered a hefty reward—but had not heard even a rumor of a species similar to hers on Mafana.

Or was it her work? He knew that she was not progressing as quickly as she had hoped, but she was experienced enough to know that answers did not appear overnight.

What if it was him? No matter how eagerly she welcomed

him into her body, or how sweetly she curled against him as she slept, he had the uneasy suspicion that she was withholding part of herself from him.

Instead of heading for his study as he planned, he went to the kitchen instead.

"Do you think something is bothering Kate?" he demanded.

Simea raised an eyebrow. "Good morning to you as well."

"I'm sorry. I'm just worried about her."

"Hmph." She bent back over the dough she was rolling out. "Why do you think something is wrong? She seems to have accepted her status happily enough."

"Her status?"

"You know, House slave."

"She is not a slave, and you know it," he said angrily. "She is a free female."

"Is she?" Simea studied him thoughtfully. "She is not Mafanan, which means she has few rights under our laws. She has no credits, no property, nothing of her own. Freedom means very little without those things."

"She doesn't need any of that. I will provide everything that she needs. That she wants."

"So she is at your mercy? That doesn't sound much better than slavery to me."

He gave her a horrified look, and she sighed. "You're a good boy, A'tai, but you've grown up surrounded by wealth and privilege. You've no idea what it is like to be at the mercy of others. Your family was very good to me, but I always knew I could be turned away at any moment."

"We would never—"

"Perhaps not," she admitted. "But the possibility was there. My family was very poor, and I saved every penny I earned until I was sure that I could support them. And then I saved more in case the storms came."

"I would never permit such storms to damage her," he protested, then sighed. "Do you truly think that she is worried about her future?"

Simea turned back to her dough. "The only way to know is to talk to her."

"She says everything is fine."

"Well, there you are."

"But I don't think it is."

She sighed. "A'tai, you are a grown male. Talk to your female and leave me out of it."

"Yes, ma'am," he said meekly, and headed back to his study, still turning over her words.

He found it hard to believe that Kate had so little faith in him that she was worried about the future, but what if Simea was right? He picked up his scroll, but he couldn't concentrate. At last he sighed and put it down, then called his senior steward.

Once he set things in motion—over his steward's protests—he was finally able to relax and concentrate on his work.

The documents arrived a week later, along with a message from his mother demanding he return to the palace. She had been growing increasingly impatient, and he knew that at some point he would have to go back. Would Kate enjoy Kapenta, he wondered. Perhaps it would distract her from whatever was worrying her.

Although most of the time she was her usual fascinating self, he still caught those odd moments of unhappiness. He had decided that Simea must be right, and he could hardly wait until tonight to relieve her mind. He arranged for dinner on the patio outside their room. When she came out to join him, she was wearing the sheer pink gown Simea had given him that first day.

The lamplight shimmered on the fabric, turning it even

more transparent as the evening breeze lifted it around her body in a cloud of silk. Her dark locks floated in the same breeze. His moa threatened to emerge as she came towards him, her nipples rosy little points beneath the fabric. He was tempted to forget about dinner and documents and take her straight to bed, but he wanted to make sure she was happy.

"Do you like this? I found it in the dressing room."

Her tone was demure but he could see the mischief sparkling in her sea green eyes and had no doubt that she noticed the flare of his arousal.

"You are a vision of loveliness."

"I must admit, I feel pretty." She shook her head. "I never thought I was the type of woman to enjoy getting dressed up."

"You could always remain undressed," he suggested helpfully, and she laughed.

"If I did, you would never let me leave our rooms."

She wasn't wrong.

"Come and sit down. I have a surprise for you."

"Oh? I'm not a big fan of surprises."

"You'll like this one," he assured her.

She gave him a suspicious look, but followed him to the table. He had intended to wait until after they had finished their meal, but he was too excited.

"Here!" He handed her the two silk-tied scrolls.

"What are these?"

"Open them."

She obeyed, then sighed. "I've only been studying Mafanan for two weeks. The learning program is very helpful, but this writing is so ornate. Does this one say something about a house? I don't understand the other one at all."

"This one is the deed to this house. I have placed it in your name."

"I don't understand."

"And this is an account that I have opened in your name. So that you have funds of your own."

Her mouth trembled. "Why would I need that?"

"In case I am not around."

Her face turned pale. "You're leaving me?"

"No, of course not. I just wanted you to feel secure. To know that you would be provided for."

"When you leave me."

"Why do you keep saying that?" he roared. "I'm not leaving you, and you're not leaving me."

She didn't seem to hear him. "It's all right. I already figured it out. I know it can't last."

"My amali, I have no idea what you are talking about."

To his horror, her eyes filled with tears. "You were right. I am deadly."

"Oh, for fuck's sake."

He snatched her out of her chair and carried her through into the bedroom. He clasped her arms and legs, spreading her out beneath him, waiting for her body to relax into his grip. Tears still filled her eyes, but he saw her nipples bead.

"Now, my Kate, explain to me why you are distressed."

She licked her lips, but didn't answer him. He inserted another limb between her legs, circling her eager little clit, but not touching it. She tried to lift her hips but he held her tighter. Her sweetness flooded his suckers and he had to remind himself why they were in this position.

"Why do you think we will not last?"

When she still hesitated, he brushed lightly across her swollen clit.

"A'tai! Please."

"Tell me."

"You want children," she burst out.

"Of course." He frowned down at her. "And you do not?"

"I would love to have children with you." A tear crept down her cheek.

"Then what is the problem?"

"I don't think it's possible. We are completely different species."

"I had not considered that," he said slowly. "We are so compatible in every way."

"Except that one." Another tear fell, and one of his limbs gently caressed her cheek, drinking in the sweetness of her sorrow.

"Then it is not to be." He felt a fleeting pang of regret that they would not share that experience, then smiled at her. "As long as I have you, I am content."

"But you have to have an heir."

"There are any number of people in my family who would be happy to be named heir," he said dryly. "Or perhaps we could adopt."

"You really don't mind?"

"No."

"And you're not going to put me aside so you can have a family with a Mafanan female?"

"That's what you thought?" He suppressed a groan as he realized how she had interpreted the documents, then leaned down until their faces were only inches apart and looked directly into her eyes. "Listen very closely. I love you, Kate. I will never put you aside. Not for a Mafanan or any other female in the galaxy."

"You really love me?"

"More than life itself."

A tremulous smile quivered on her lips. "I love you too."

Triumph roared through him as his moa prepared to emerge, but a sudden thought interrupted. He scooped her up in his arms, ignoring her faint murmur of protest, and headed for the door.

"What are you doing?" She stared up at him as he glided rapidly towards the water.

"A traditional Mafanan bonding ceremony is always consummated in the water."

"You mean have sex in the water?"

The sweetness of her arousal perfumed the air.

"Beneath the water," he corrected. "I will breathe for you."

The waves curled around his feet as they reached the ocean, but he curbed his impatience long enough to repeat the words he had uttered to her that first day in the cave.

"I will provide for you in all things and protect you against all others. I will treat you with the utmost respect. You will belong only to me. And I will belong only to you."

"I will belong only to you, and you will belong only to me." Her smile lit up her face. "I love you, A'tai."

"I love you, my Kate. Are you ready?"

"And very willing."

His mouth closed over hers as soon as she finished talking, and he sprang forward into the water. Her arms and legs wrapped around him, clinging as tightly as his limbs, and her soft little tongue stroked his. He propelled them through the water, already knowing the perfect place to take her. He just hoped he could last until then as she writhed eagerly in his arms.

A cluster of rocks formed an underwater grotto at the far end of the beach. The moon shone down into the water, turning it into green crystal. More of the susulu clung to the rocks, adding their own soft pink glow. He came to a halt in the center of the grotto, moving just enough to maintain their position as he committed every moment to memory—the soft warmth of her body, her sweetness perfuming the water, the way she clung to him and her tongue entwined with his.

Her arms tightened around his neck, and she moved restlessly against his stomach, trying to stimulate her pleasure button. He was only too happy to assist, sliding a limb between their bodies and closing firmly around the heated nub. She cried out into his mouth and more of her sweetness flooded the water. His engorged moa eagerly sipped at her essence, but he was determined not to rush this moment. He let the tip of a limb slip inside her channel instead, the exquisitely tight heat causing him to groan.

She wiggled impatiently and even though he knew it was only a sign of her impatience, his body responded instinctively, locking her into the mating position and holding her open for his penetration. He wanted to experience every part of her body from her luscious breasts to her delicious cunt. He wrapped his limbs around her, his suckers tasting every inch of her skin. As he withdrew his limb from her channel, he let the slick tip probe at the delicate pucker of her anus. She jerked, but then he felt the heat of her nectar swirling between them. Triumph filled him. He would have all of her.

And then, when they were as entwined as it was possible to be, he finally let his moa enter her. She climaxed as soon as he entered, and her hot little channel never stopped pulsing as he filled her over and over again, until his seed finally roared through his moa and exploded into her, a rush of heated ecstasy.

She continued to quiver around him as they floated in the clear green depths, still locked together. He could taste her tears, sweeter than the ocean water, even as she clung to him. He rose to the surface so that they could speak. Their lips finally parted, and she took a deep breath. Her cheeks were wet, her eyes shining, and her smile radiant.

"I love you, A'tai."

"I love you too, my Kate."

He swam slowly back to their home, completely happy as she nestled against him.

The next day, she discovered the cause of the damaged algae.

CHAPTER SEVENTEEN

Kate stared at the results of her experiment, her pulse racing. Could it be that simple?

She forced herself to go through the results again, then grinned and hurried back to the main house. A'tai was in his study as usual, but from the frown on his face, he was dealing with House matters rather than research for his paper.

"You don't look happy," she said as she entered the room.

"I'm happier now that you're here."

His smile sent a pleasant little ripple of warmth through her body.

"I have something to tell you."

"Then come here and tell me."

She went to him, but perched on the desk in front of him instead of sitting on his lap.

"It's about the algae damage. I think I know the answer," she said slowly. "Or at least I have a very strong theory."

"What is it?"

"My understanding is that you recently started using powdered tigi shells in the nutrients used to feed the algae."

"Yes, but I don't see how it could be a factor. We started using them five years ago, and the algae damage didn't begin until this year. And it's a common practice. Most of the Houses have started doing the same because it's an efficient use of resources."

"It is, but the problem is that the tigi shells contain trace amounts of a bacteria which can harm the algae. It takes time—a long time—before it builds up in sufficient quantities to cause damage, but eventually it reaches the point where it overwhelms the algae's natural immunity."

He frowned thoughtfully. "Are you sure about this?"

"As sure as I can be under the circumstances."

"Why has it not affected the other Houses?"

"Would they tell you if it had?" she asked dryly. She had gathered enough over the past few weeks to recognize the competition that existed between the Houses.

He shrugged. "Perhaps not directly, but only a few of them have shown any decrease in what they are offering for sale."

"I would guess that the ones with less to offer are also southern Houses."

He considered the matter, then nodded. "You're correct. Why does that matter?"

"Because the warmer the temperatures, the faster the bacteria grow. It will affect all of them eventually, but it will take longer. You can see it on a smaller scale on your own farms. Remember how the beds on the sunny side of the bay have a higher occurrence of the damage?"

"Is the damage irreversible?"

"I don't think so. In fact, I don't even think that you will need to stop using the tigi shells completely. However, you won't be able to apply them every year. It will take some experimentation to discover the appropriate frequency."

A startled look suddenly crossed his face, and she raised her eyebrows. "What is it?"

"As you were talking, I thought it sounded familiar. I just realized why. Our people have farmed algae for many, many generations, and the process is described in some of the older scrolls. They always let a bed lie fallow every third year. We abandoned that process once we discovered more powerful nutrients, but perhaps they were right all along."

"We have a saying back on Earth—those who don't learn from history are doomed to repeat it." She smiled triumphantly at him.

He laughed and tugged her into his arms. "Unless they also have a very clever mate. Have you told Pulata?"

She shook her head, well aware that despite his concessions, he wasn't happy with her working so closely with the other male. "I wanted to talk to you first. We'll need to test the bacteria levels in the remaining beds. The ones with the highest counts will need to be harvested immediately and then left fallow."

"Can they be cleansed?"

"Possibly. Although we would need to be careful to make sure we aren't simply spreading the problem elsewhere."

She tapped her finger against her lips, already considering possible solutions. He brought her attention back to him by removing her finger and replacing it with his mouth. He kissed her until she was clinging to him, then raised his head.

"I'm afraid this means we will have to return to the capital."

Her heart skipped a beat. Even though he had assured her that he was doing everything he could to find her friends, she kept wondering if there were additional possibilities in a more populous environment. On the other hand, she was happier here on the island than she had ever been. And she knew he was happy as well. Would that change once he was back in the city and had to assume a more active role in House affairs? She strongly suspected he had come to the island in order to avoid just that.

"Why do we need to go?" she asked.

"I think it is a message best served in person," he said slowly. "The other Houses will be suspicious, especially since this will impact their yield."

"If they don't monitor it, that will happen anyway," she pointed out.

"I know. And I'm almost tempted to let them discover it for themselves, but it would not be fair to their people. Algae products form a large part of the diet for many of the poorer families."

"Then I guess we're going to Kapenta."

"Yes." He hesitated. "This means you will have to meet my mother."

Oh, joy. Nothing she had heard from him, or Simea, had encouraged her to look forward to the prospect.

"What are you going to tell her? About us?"

"The truth, of course."

"How do you think she's going to react?" Based on everything he had said—and not said, she didn't think it would be a positive reaction.

"I don't know," he admitted. "But she will have to accept the truth sooner or later."

"Then I suppose it might as well be sooner."

"I will arrange for some gowns for you." He held up a hand before she could speak. "I'm sure you're about to tell me to make them practical, but it will be necessary to wear more decorative clothes while we're there."

She sighed and nodded. "I understand."

"And of course, you're still welcome to go without clothing when we're alone."

The warmth in his eyes sent a resulting quiver through her system. "I'll consider that option."

Less than two days later, they stood together on the bow of his boat as they approached Kapenta. She gave a sigh of relief at the sight. Her stomach had not responded well to the trip, and she was looking forward to solid ground beneath her feet again.

She leaned forward eagerly to inspect the city. She wasn't quite sure what she had expected, but it wasn't these ornate and vaguely Mediterranean buildings. It reminded her somewhat of Venice, she decided, with the low-slung brightly colored buildings and the elaborate stonework. The city was strung out over a series of islands, connected by decorative bridges. Small colorful boats darted back and forth between the islands. Nothing about it would have made her think it was an interstellar port.

But even if she thought that, she saw a spaceship descend from the sky and land somewhere in the interior of one of the islands. Her heart skipped a beat. Despite A'tai's assurances, she couldn't help worrying that the slavers would come looking for her, or that the mysterious Royal Fleet would take her away from him.

A'tai put a reassuring arm around her waist, and she looked up to see him smiling down at her. "You're safe with me, amali."

"My heart knows that, but my brain can conjure up a lot of possibilities."

"You know I have a remedy for that busy brain of yours."

"Yes, but I don't think this is exactly the place."

"Perhaps not," he conceded. "Although I could order everyone below."

"Can you order everyone off the docks as well?" They were approaching a busy landing teeming with people.

"Actually, yes. That is the private dock of House Maulimu. This is the edge of our property, and the palace extends down around that curve and onto the next island."

"Oh." Her stomach fluttered as she took in the long, elaborate façade. Although most of the building was only three stories high, it seemed to stretch on for miles. Even though she had seen the castle on Ataian, and even though she was becoming familiar with the amount of work he did, most of the time they had been together, it had been just the two of them. Knowing that he was a prince intellectually wasn't quite the same as seeing the full extent of his position.

"Maybe I shouldn't have come with you," she muttered.

Her fingers knotted in the embroidered fabric of her gown, and he put a reassuring hand over them. "Then I would not have come either. I will not be separated from you, my Kate."

His words made her feel a little better, but as the boat docked and he helped her ashore, she could feel the eyes upon them. Everyone bowed as he passed, but although he nodded his head in acknowledgment, he didn't stop to speak to anyone.

They walked through a set of wide double doors into an airy, two-story hall. A wall of windows overlooked the sea, while open archways led off to the sides on both levels. People bustled around the space, but it was considerably less crowded than the docks, and she breathed a sigh of relief. A'tai stopped, and looked down at her.

"I think it's best that I talk to my mother immediately. Would you prefer that I take you to our quarters first or do you want to come with me now?"

She was tempted to take the coward's way out and avoid the visit, but she would have to face his mother sooner or later. It might as well be sooner.

"I'll come with you," she decided.

He pulled her against his side, and even though she was aware of more speculative glances, the familiar position made her feel more comfortable. She took a deep breath. "I'm ready."

He walked briskly along a wide corridor, then through a series of increasingly elaborate rooms, most of them filled with Mafanan females, all of them richly dressed. The embroidered gown that had seemed so ornate earlier suddenly seemed extraordinarily plain.

"Who are all these people?" she murmured softly.

"My mother's attendants. She doesn't like being alone." He shrugged. "She also sends them out to run errands and gather gossip. There is very little that occurs in Kapenta that she does not know about."

"Does that mean she knows about us?"

"If she didn't before, she did as soon as we stepped off the boat. Although she will undoubtedly pretend to be surprised."

He proved to be correct. A flustered servant attempted to tell him that his mother wasn't receiving, but A'tai ignored him and led her into a beautiful, spacious room. Every detail was exquisite, from the fragile decorative furniture in shades of pale pink to the beautifully woven tapestries that covered the walls. But all of it was designed to complement the female reclining gracefully on a couch carefully placed in an enormous bay window.

"I'm so sorry to disturb you, Mother," A'tai said sardonically. "But since you have been demanding my return, I assumed you would want to see me immediately."

"You really have no consideration for my well-being," the female said in a faint, plaintive voice.

As they drew closer, Kate decided she would have recognized the female as A'tai's mother under any circumstances. There was a distinct family resemblance, starting with the golden eyes. But unlike the warmth in A'tai's eyes, his mother surveyed her disdainfully and immediately dismissed her.

Even her features were a more feminine version of A'tai's, and Kate had seen enough Mafanan females to realize that she was extremely attractive. A long, shimmering gown accentuated her slender figure, and Kate suddenly felt short, dumpy and all too obviously human.

"Did you resolve the problem?" The female asked A'tai, ignoring Kate completely.

"No, but my mate did. Mother, this is Kate. Kate, this is my mother U'rsul."

"I'm pleased to meet you," she lied, sternly resisting the impulse to bob a curtsy.

"Your mate? What kind of foolishness is this? You cannot possibly be telling me that you have bonded with an offworlder."

Despite U'rsul's exaggerated shock, Kate decided she wasn't in the least bit surprised.

"That is exactly what I am telling you."

"Don't be ridiculous."

A'tai sighed. "Mother, I did not come here to argue with you. Kate and I are bonded, and you will treat her with the respect which she deserves. Now, why was it so urgent that I return?"

"You know it really upsets me when you speak to me so gruffly."

"Mother, we've had a long trip. Is there something we need to discuss or not?"

"We are having guests for dinner tonight."

"That's it? Another dinner party?"

"I have made certain... arrangements." Her voice dropped meaningfully. "As we discussed before you left."

"To which I did not agree, and which are now no longer relevant," A'tai said firmly.

U'rsul assumed a martyred expression. "It's far too late to change the plans without incurring a great deal of ill will."

"We will just have to take that chance. Now I am going to take Kate to our quarters. When do the... festivities commence?"

"We are gathering for cocktails on the terrace at sunset."

"Then we will see you there."

He inclined his head, tightened his hold on Kate, and headed for the door.

"We need to talk before then, A'tai. Privately." U'rsul called after them. For a female with such a fragile demeanor, she could certainly make her voice heard.

"I will try and find the time," A'tai said and kept walking.

CHAPTER EIGHTEEN

As soon as they were outside U'rsul's room, Kate saw a gaggle of females rush back through the doors. A'tai snorted.

"Her second audience, no doubt ready to be shocked and horrified by her ungrateful son."

"Do you really think she's going to—"

"Regale them with a story of how rudely I treated her? Of course."

He led her through another door and into a corridor lined with windows overlooking the sea. Only a few people were in sight, and her shoulders finally started to relax.

"So what did you think of my mother's little performance?" he asked.

"What do you mean?"

"Her shock at your presence. The carefully staged scene—she is never alone unless she chooses to be. She started setting that up as soon as we got off the boat."

"I don't think she likes me very much," she said, a little

regretfully. She had held out a distant hope that his mother wouldn't be as bad as she had imagined.

He shrugged. "I don't think she likes me very much either. I'm not sure she really likes anyone, although she is more inclined to pretend with others."

"What about your father? Did she like him?"

"I honestly don't know. He was devoted to her, waiting on her hand and foot. It was one of the reasons why I was determined not to become involved with a female."

"I think it's a little too late for that now," she said dryly. "Do you regret it?"

He immediately halted, pressing her against the wall and looming over her. "You are well aware that I do not. And the fact that I was so cautious meant that I was waiting for you when you came to me."

The familiar pulse of arousal began low in her stomach, but all he did was drop a brief kiss on her lips, before resuming their walk.

He shook his head, obviously still thinking about his parents' relationship. "But even though I have my doubts about the two of them, they certainly spent a lot of time together. And she was... different when he was around."

"Perhaps she loved him just as much," Kate said, trying to be fair.

"Perhaps."

He didn't sound convinced, but they had reached another set of doors at the end of the corridor and he dropped the subject. He waved his hand over a hidden panel and the doors unlocked, the high-tech lock at odds with the ancient stonework. Once inside, he paused in a circular entry hall with an inlaid marble floor and a delicate metal staircase curving gracefully up one wall. Arches opened from the hall into the surrounding rooms.

"These are our quarters. The living room and dining room are on this level. My study and our bedroom above. Guest rooms on the top floor." He hesitated. "You are welcome to change anything you do not like, but I was wondering if you would like a laboratory."

"How long are we going to be here?"

He sighed. "I don't really know. I need to spread the word about the nutrient issue, and attend some Council meetings. We will probably need to attend some social events as well."

Her heart sank. She had hoped this was to be a short visit, but she suspected it was going to stretch out. "In that case, probably."

"I'll see about having one of the guest rooms converted." A Mafanan male came gliding into the room as he finished speaking. "Ah, Uauna. I have a project for you."

"Yes, sire."

"This is my bond mate, Lady Kate."

Uauna bowed without batting an eye. "I am very pleased to meet you, Lady Kate."

"She is a scientist, and she will need a laboratory while we are here. I thought perhaps the front guest room."

"Of course, sire. Do you have a list of requirements, Lady Kate?"

"Contact Warden Pulata," A'tai said before she could answer. "He equipped her lab on Ataian so he can tell you what is needed."

"Yes sire. Is there anything else you require? I have a light meal waiting in the dining room."

"Thank you, Uauna. That will be all for now."

"It was nice to meet you," Kate said.

Uauna bowed and whisked himself out of the room, and she turned to glare at A'tai. "You know I am quite capable of talking for myself."

"I'm sorry, amali. I just wanted to get rid of him so I could have you to myself."

Her annoyance vanished as he lifted her in his arms and started kissing her. By the time he raised his head, his skin was glimmering gold and her own body was humming with arousal.

"Are you hungry?" he growled.

Her stomach still felt uneasy, but she wouldn't have cared if she was starving when he looked at her like that. "Not for food."

"Good." He lifted her into his arms and carried her up the elaborate staircase and into the bedroom.

A'TAI CAREFULLY ADJUSTED THE BEDROOM CURTAINS so that the Sisters' low afternoon rays would not disturb his sleeping mate. As much as he hated to do it, he had decided that it would be better to confront his mother now and find out exactly what she was scheming this time. He pulled on a formal robe and glided softly out of the room.

Uauna appeared as he reached the bottom of the stairs. "Sire, your mother has—"

"Sent numerous messages?"

Uauna nodded, and A'tai sighed.

"Don't worry. I'm going to see her now. My mate is sleeping, but if she awakens before I return, please tell her that I will be back shortly."

"Yes sire. I will also have another meal ready. I noticed that you did not have a chance to partake. No doubt you had other matters to attend to."

Uauna's face was as bland as ever, but A'tai thought there was a twinkle in his eye. He laughed.

"You are correct. Please make sure that there is something

available for Lady Kate if she is hungry. She likes fruit, and she prefers cooked fish."

"Yes, sire. I took the liberty of contacting nurse Simea to ascertain her preferences."

"You are as efficient as ever, Uauna. Thank you."

"You're welcome, sire. And may I be so forward as to offer my congratulations? You have been alone for a long time."

"My mate was worth waiting for."

"Yes, sire. The House will celebrate your happiness."

A'tai went on his way, encouraged by his valet's sincere congratulations. His mother was nowhere near as receptive.

"You cannot possibly be serious about this." U'rsul was so agitated that she was actually pacing back and forth. "A little indulgence with an offworlder female isn't unexpected. Even your father wasn't immune to their charms, especially if they were pretty and helpless, but—"

"Wait. What did you just say about Father?"

"You didn't know that he occasionally indulged himself elsewhere?"

He had the oddest sensation that the room was spinning. His father, the one who had always appeared so completely devoted to his mother, had not been faithful to her?

"You allowed this?"

Pain flashed across her face so quickly that he could almost convince himself he hadn't seen it. "I did not have a choice. I decided to be grateful that he never indulged with a Mafanan female."

He had no idea what to say. He couldn't even imagine the possibility of desiring a female other than his Kate.

"But as I was saying," his mother continued. "You do not bond with an offworlder. If you absolutely insist on keeping her, you can install her as your concubine, but you must choose a formal mate from another House."

"Don't you think this theoretical female from another House would object to that?"

She shrugged. "Not if she was brought up correctly. And as soon as she provides us with an heir, she would be free to do the same."

"No female of mine will ever stray!" he roared.

"You are really behaving in the most primitive fashion. The sooner you put this female aside, the better."

"Mother, I'm going to say this one more time. I have chosen Kate and she has chosen me. We are bonded and there is absolutely nothing you can say or do which is going to change that."

She gave him a speculative look, and he dreaded to think what was going through her mind.

"If you try to interfere between us—in any way—I will have you removed from this palace and banished to the northern territories."

"You would not!"

Despite her outrage, she actually looked uncertain. *Good.*

"I assure you that I would." Although he would vastly prefer not to do so, if she did anything to hurt Kate, he wouldn't hesitate.

Her martyred expression reappeared. "Then you will need to talk to Lord F'tonu tonight and find some way to convince him that choosing an offworlder female over his daughter is not the greatest of insults."

She had a point, but...

"You were the one who approached him, not me."

She lifted a graceful shoulder. "But I was approaching him on behalf of the House."

"Fine," he sighed. "I will talk to him."

"Good. And if there's any chance of preserving the trade connection to Honara, it would be to our advantage."

He couldn't help but admire how quickly she switched from outraged female to ruthless businessperson.

"Agreed. Now, if that is all, I will see you tonight."

"If you are bringing your female, I assume you have arranged for appropriate clothing?"

When he hesitated, she sighed. "I will send something. We do not want her disgracing the House."

"She could be clothed in rags and she would still not disgrace the House," he growled.

For the briefest moment, her face softened and she nodded.

He bowed and turned to leave. He was almost at the door when he decided he had to know.

"Did you do it, mother? Find someone to occupy your time after I was born?"

He half expected her to be outraged by the question, but after a long silence, she simply shook her head. "No. I loved him."

CHAPTER NINETEEN

"Are you sure I look all right?" Kate whispered as they approached the Grand Terrace.

"You look beautiful. Now stop fidgeting."

Despite his instruction, she nervously adjusted the dress again. She had never worn anything so beautiful.

Shortly after she had awoken from her nap, A'tai had returned from having spoken to his mother. He looked oddly thoughtful but assured her there was nothing to worry about. They sat down to a light meal containing many of her favorites, but she was too nervous to eat. He was frowning at her when they were interrupted by a swarm of females who had swept her away with them.

The fact that A'tai 's mother had sent them did not reassure her, but they turned out to be surprisingly friendly, if inclined to bouts of giggling. They had arranged her hair in an elaborate updo, studded with jewels, murmuring all the while at the fine texture of her hair. A shimmering gold powder had been applied to her face and the rest of her body. Before she had a chance to object, they'd stripped off her gown, and replaced it with the one she was currently wearing. More giggling had ensued as they tried to figure out how to make the gown lie smoothly over her breasts. In the end, the head female had given the graceful Mafanan shrug.

"It is not perhaps the most elegant line, but I suspect that the Prince will not care."

Based on his reaction when he saw her, the female was quite correct. The deep green gown matched her eyes, but fine golden threads shimmered in the delicate fabric. In typical Mafanan fashion, the skirt was slit on both sides from her ankles to her hip, the opening accented with intricate gold embroidery. More embroidery framed the open neckline that plunged almost to her waist. On a Mafanan female, it would simply have revealed a swath of smooth skin. On her, it highlighted the inside curves of her breasts.

A'tai 's eyes had heated at the sight of her, but then he frowned. "I did not consider the fact that our fashion would be so revealing."

"Do you think I should change?" she asked nervously.

She suspected he would have liked to say yes, but in the end he shook his head. "No. It is an appropriate outfit, and you look beautiful. But you will remain at my side, understand?"

She had nodded, already deciding to stick to him like glue. But as they stepped out onto the Grand Terrace, she realized she hadn't anticipated the sheer number of people present. There must have been more than a hundred people milling around on the expanse of marble overlooking the water. Flowering plants formed graceful arbors over small seating areas, while discreet servants passed through the crowd carrying trays of delicacies. Although most of those present were Mafanan, she was not the only alien present. Two leonine males were arguing in a corner while a red skinned male with the disturbing resemblance to a devil entertained a group of females hanging on his every word. There were a few other faces in the crowd that weren't Mafanan, and she relaxed a little.

A'tai circulated easily, exchanging brief comments with many of those present although he was far more arrogant than he usually was when they were alone. He always introduced her as his mate, and no one ever questioned it, although she caught more than one speculative glance.

And then they ran into a large, rather stocky Mafanan male accompanied by a very pretty young female. The male glowered at A'tai.

"Lord F'tonu, what a pleasant surprise," A'tai said smoothly. "May I introduce my mate, Lady Kate?"

Lord F'tonu's mouth opened, but before he could speak, the girl stepped forward. "I'm very pleased to meet you, Lady Kate. I am E'lofi."

The girl's smile looked genuine enough, and Kate returned it. "It's nice to meet you too."

"Prince A'tai, I really must protest—" the male started.

"I do not believe this is the appropriate location for this conversation," A'tai said coldly. He cast a quick, apologetic look at Kate. "If you would care to accompany me to my study…"

The male looked over at the girl and she gave him a sunny smile. "Don't worry about me, Papa. Lady Kate and I will get better acquainted."

A'tai didn't look thrilled by her words, but Lord F'tonu was already storming off and he reluctantly followed him. The girl laughed.

"Males. Always puffing up their chests." She gave a quick look around, then stepped closer to Kate. "You do realize we're the center of attention, don't you?"

She could feel the eyes practically burning into her. "Yes, but why?"

"Because your mate was supposed to bond with me."

The ground rocked beneath Kate's feet, and E'lofi quickly put her arm through Kate's.

"I'm sorry. That was stupid of me. Why don't we go find someplace to talk?"

Kate really didn't want to go anywhere with the pretty Mafanan girl, but she wanted to get away from all the staring eyes. She managed a nod, and E'lofi somehow managed to move them quickly and gracefully through the crowd and into a small curtained nook with two chairs overlooking the water.

"There, that's better." E'lofi giggled. "I always try to find somewhere private at a party. You never know when it will be needed."

Kate sank down on the nearest chair, her knees feeling oddly weak.

"You really didn't know, did you?" E'lofi asked.

"No. He never said anything."

"I'm not sure how much he knew." The girl gave her a sympathetic look. "I think it was mainly between his mother and my father."

Kate thought back over some of the things that A'tai had said, or rather had not said. "I think he knew."

Jealousy roared through her as she looked at E'lofi. She was so young and pretty and graceful. A'tai wouldn't need to breathe for her if they swam together, and she would be able to give him children. The last thought hurt the most.

"You had an arrangement?" she asked stiffly.

"No, no. Nothing that formal. My father and his mother were simply discussing the possibilities."

"I'm... sorry."

"I'm not!" E'lofi grinned. "I know I'll have to mate with someone one day, but I'm in no hurry. And, no offense, I would never have chosen Prince A'tai."

The ground rocked again. How could any female in her right mind not want A'tai?

"You didn't want to marry—I mean, bond with him?" she asked, trying to conceal her shock.

"No. I mean he's very handsome, of course, but he's very... intense."

She wasn't wrong.

E'lofi's face turned dreamy. "I would prefer a more casual mate, someone who will let me be me."

"A'tai wouldn't try and change you," Kate said, then wondered why she was arguing.

"Not on purpose perhaps, but I'm not good at asserting myself. I would end up as little more than his shadow. I'm not like you."

"I suspect I've had more practice asserting myself. Although it occurs to me that you're doing a pretty good job of being independent right now."

E'lofi giggled. "I usually manage to get what I want, but I don't want to have to fight for it every time."

No, Kate decided. A union between the two of them would not have gone well. She wondered if the other female realized that if A'tai had loved her, he would have been putty in her hands. Despite the girl's sweetness, she suspected that she could be as manipulative as his mother.

"Then all's well that ends well," she said aloud. "How will your father react?"

"He'll growl and carry on," E'lofi said easily. "But he'll get over it. He loves me."

"I'm glad he won't cause you any problems."

E'lofi giggled again. "Actually, I think he'll roar so much tonight that he'll feel really guilty tomorrow. He'll probably send me shopping just to ease his guilt." She tilted her head.

"Would you like to come? If you're staying in the capital for a while, you'll need more clothes."

"Really?"

"Oh, yes. It would cause quite a scandal if Prince A'tai's wife wore the same outfit on more than one occasion."

She was beginning to understand why A'tai preferred to avoid the city, but she wouldn't mind a few more dresses and E'lofi was turning out to be surprisingly good company.

"Why not?" she said. "If your father sends you, I'll be happy to accompany you."

"He will," E'lofi assured her. "Now we'd better return to the terrace, arm in arm like the good friends we've become."

Kate laughed and took her arm. She could hardly wait to see U'rsul's reaction.

They returned to the terrace to find that A'tai and Lord F'tonu had returned. A'tai was scanning the crowd anxiously searching for her. Both he and Lord F'tonu hurried over as soon as they spotted them.

"Is everything all right, my Kate?"

"Yes, I think so. But we need to talk later."

He winced and nodded, just as a bell chimed.

"What does that mean?"

"Time for the banquet," he said grimly. "I'm afraid we should stay."

When they entered the vast dining room, Kate was assigned a seat far from A'tai's—no doubt his mother's doing. He looked outraged, and she could tell he was prepared to go to war, but she put her hand on his arm and shook her head.

"It's fine. It's just a dinner."

"Are you sure? I will have the entire room rearranged if necessary."

"Don't worry about it."

He scowled but escorted her to her seat, frowning suspiciously at the males on either side of her. Since even she could tell that both of them were clearly elderly, he relaxed a little, giving her a quick kiss before he went off to take his own seat. Somehow she was not surprised to see E'lofi seated at his side. The girl made some laughing comment, and he smiled reluctantly. The sight made her chest ache, and she resolutely refused to look in that direction again.

Despite the inauspicious beginning, the dinner turned out to be surprisingly pleasant. The male to her left was only interested in his food, but the male to her right turned out to be a scientist acquainted with Warden Pulata. He was familiar with the issue with the algae, and delighted to hear the results of her experiments. The food didn't suit her so she ignored it and spent the rest of the meal discussing some of the unique properties of the Mafanan oceans with him. They were still deep in discussion when a firm hand closed over her shoulder. She jumped, then looked up to see A'tai glaring at her companion.

"The meal is over, Enetisi. I have come to reclaim my mate."

"Yes, yes, of course. We've had a most fascinating discussion. I have invited Lady Kate to come and visit my laboratory."

"We were only in the city for a short visit. I'm not sure that she will have time."

He had her out of her chair and halfway across the dining room before she could do more than wave a goodbye to Enetisi.

"Why are you being so rude?" she demanded.

"I did not like the way he was looking at you."

"You have got to be kidding. We were simply discussing the biological composition of your oceans. And he's an old man!"

"A male is never too old to appreciate a beautiful female."

"The way you were appreciating E'lofi?"

The astonishment on his face did much to ease her lingering jealousy. "E'lofi? She's a silly child."

"A very pretty child. And actually, I don't think she's silly at all."

"You know that you are the only female that I am interested in, amali."

"So you aren't going to mate with her?"

He stumbled, and she hid a smile.

"No, I wasn't." She waited expectantly, and he sighed. "But my mother had proposed such a match."

"Would you have gone ahead with it?"

"I don't know. I was not in favor of the idea—which is the main reason that I was headed to Ataian. Since that is how I discovered you, perhaps we should be grateful to my mother for suggesting it."

She laughed. "I don't think I'm prepared to go that far." After a moment's hesitation, she added, "But you would have done it, wouldn't you? If I hadn't come along?"

"I would love to be able to tell you no, but I truly don't know. I do know that if I had, it would have been a business arrangement, nothing more."

"She could give you children," she said softly.

"But she is not you. I belong to you, Kate, remember?"

"And I belong to you."

Music sounded from the ballroom, and she could see people beginning to move gracefully across the floor.

"Should we attend the ball?"

"I'm afraid so. But we do not need to stay long."

"I don't really know how to dance," she whispered.

"Then it will be my pleasure to teach you."

CHAPTER TWENTY

A'tai fumed as he carried his mate back to their quarters. He should have known better than to return to Kapenta, or to have allowed his mother to dress Kate in such a provocative outfit. As soon as they had entered the ballroom, other males swarmed around her.

"You can put me down now," Kate said from her position over his shoulder.

"No."

"You're overreacting. One little dance—"

"It was two dances, and I saw the way he was looking at you," he growled.

He had been forced to dance with Lady P'tris— who was old enough to be his grandmother—only to return and find Kate twirling merrily around the dance floor in the arms of a Kaisarian prince. When he had tried to reclaim her, he had been waylaid by people wanting to offer their congratulations.

"He was telling me that the new Emperor's mate is human. Is that true?"

"I don't know, and I don't care." His hand clamped down

even tighter on her delightfully round ass and felt her wiggle against him.

But he had every intention of finding out. If it was true, how many males would decide that having a human mate might ingratiate them with the new Emperor? Would they come looking for his female? He would never let his mate go, not even to the Emperor himself.

His instincts demanded that he assert his claim on his female, but they were still in a public area. He refused to let anyone see more of her luscious body than had already been revealed by the incredibly sensual dress. Although it did have one advantage... He adjusted his grip, letting his hand slide into the opening high on her hip so he could touch her soft skin directly.

He heard her breath catch as he touched her damp, silky curls.

"A'tai, you're acting like a caveman," she protested, but she pressed into his hand.

"There are no caves in Kapenta." He slammed through the doors to his quarters and raced up the stairs.

"It means you're acting like a primitive male," she gasped as he threw her down on their bed.

"I feel like a primitive male," he growled as he loomed over her.

The dark green gown was an erotic contrast to her pale skin, as dark as his moa when he entered her, and her skin shimmered with golden powder as if reflecting her arousal. Her nipples thrust against the silky fabric, so close to the deep neckline that a single movement would reveal them to his hungry gaze. He pushed the fabric aside, his mouth watering as the tight buds were revealed, already swollen and waiting.

He could not resist, leaning down to pull a rosy nub into his mouth. She arched into his touch, and his limbs stirred, anxious to restrain her, but he wanted her free to prove that she wanted him as much as he wanted her. He curled his tongue around that taut peak and tugged, and she buried her hands in the thick strands of his hair, pulling him closer.

"You are mine, amali," he growled against the damp flesh and felt her shiver.

"Yes."

He kissed his way down her soft stomach, then waited for her to spread her thighs. Her legs quivered, and then she slowly parted them, revealing her flushed folds, already glistening with arousal. He ran his tongue through the sweetness, then concentrated on her pleasure bud as she shook beneath him. One of his limbs slid into her channel and her body arched so violently he was almost dislodged, but still he did not restrain her into the mating position.

He looked up at her as more of his limbs curled around her swollen nipples.

"Are you going to fight me, Kate?"

Her eyes were dazed with pleasure, and he saw her struggle to focus on his words. "What?"

"Are you going to fight me?" His limb slipped free, seeking her tight bottom hole.

"Why would—oh my God."

More arousal coated his tongue as his tip entered the tiny channel. His moa was so engorged that the mere brush of the sheets was agonizing.

"Are you going to fight me?" he asked a third time.

"No. Why do you keep asking?" His question finally penetrated and she frowned up at him.

"Because I want to know that you will give yourself to me. Completely. Willingly. Without restraints."

He saw the understanding on her face.

"Completely. Willingly. Without restraints," she repeated. "I love you, A'tai."

He surged inside her, her incredibly tight cunt made even tighter by his limb filling her bottom hole. But she was the one holding on to him. She was the one pulling him closer. She was the one locking him against her body as his climax roared over him and hers echoed it in an endless wave of pleasure.

His jealousy was forgotten as he pressed soft kisses to every part of her body he could reach.

Her eyes were still closed, but her lips curved as she spoke.

"Okay. You can be a caveman whenever you want."

The next morning, A'tai returned to his quarters feeling tired and grouchy. Last night had been immensely pleasurable, and he had wanted to spend the morning in bed with his mate. Instead he'd been forced to leave her in order to attend a tedious breakfast meeting, followed by a meeting with the other Houses concerning the algae issue—which had not gone well, but at least it was done. If they chose not to listen, it was no longer his problem. Perhaps he could still join Kate in bed...

No, he decided after glancing at the Sisters. She would be up by now. Of course, that didn't mean he couldn't persuade her back into it. Possibly even repeat the exquisite experience of the previous evening...

When he couldn't find her in his study or the living room or the small dining area, he decided she must still be in bed. It had been a late night after all. His moa throbbed in anticipation as he slipped through the bedroom door. But the curtains were open, an untouched morning meal on the table by the window, and the bed empty. His mate had disappeared.

"Uauna!" he roared.

KATE AND THE KRAKEN

. . .

The shopping expedition was turning out to be surprisingly enjoyable, Kate decided. A message had arrived from E'lofi not long after A'tai had left. Uauna had delivered the message and sent a very young, wide-eyed maid to help her dress. He had also helpfully provided her with a small coin purse.

"I wasn't really going to buy anything," she said, trying to refuse. "Although I do have some kind of funds..."

At A'tai's insistence she had accepted the account he had offered her, as well as the deed to the farmhouse, but she had no idea how to access it.

Uauna waved a dismissive hand. "Any major purchases will of course be charged to House Maulimu. This is simply for any small purchases you should wish to make."

"But..."

"You do not wish to disgrace the House," he said firmly, and she sighed and took the purse.

She found E'lofi waiting for her in the forecourt of the palace, accompanied by two very large, imposing males.

"My bodyguards," the girl explained. "It's quite unnecessary but Papa insists, right, Leatino?"

"Yes, miss."

"I thought we would start with clothing," E'lofi continued, scanning Kate's outfit.

"Am I dressed inappropriately?"

"You look very nice," the other female said quickly, and Kate decided that meant yes.

"What's wrong with it?"

"That shade was more popular last season, and hemlines have changed. But it's quite acceptable," E'lofi added hastily.

Kate sighed. After an entire lifetime of paying little attention to her clothes other than making sure they were clean, this wasn't going to be easy.

"I really don't know much about fashion," she confessed.

"Don't worry. I'm an expert." E'lofi laughed as they started walking, the two bodyguards falling in behind them. "And the gown you wore last night was divine."

"U'rsul sent it."

"Really? She must like you."

"I think it's more likely she was afraid I would disgrace the House."

"Perhaps. She does have exquisite taste." E'lofi gave her an impish smile. "But so do I."

The seamstress E'lofi took her to turned out to be very friendly. Faiofu didn't even bat an eye at the fact that Kate was human.

"I'm quite used to offworlders," she said airily. "Although it will be a pleasant change to dress one for our social events. Now I propose five or six tea gowns to begin with, an equal number of morning robes, and of course, the ball gowns. Nothing too elaborate, I think. It would be impossible to disguise your figure so we'll accentuate it instead. Simple fabrics, perhaps, designed to follow your curves."

"That seems like a lot of clothes," Kate said, overwhelmed by the prospect.

E'lofi and Faiofu laughed.

"It's only the beginning," E'lofi assured her. "Assuming you intend to participate in the season?"

"I'm not really sure." *I hope not.*

It turned out that the seamstress's idea of simple fabrics was not the same as Kate's. But despite her doubts, it was easy to get swept away in the excitement as the beautiful materials were draped over her body, then pinned and tucked to determine the most flattering lines. Overwhelmed by the sheer number and variety of options, she let E'lofi and Faiofu make most of the decisions. Nothing as vulgar as cost was ever mentioned, but she left suspecting they had spent quite a lot of A'tai's money.

"Now that you've seen one of our most exclusive shops, you should experience the other side," E'lofi said cheerfully. "Let's go to the market."

"Miss E'lofi," Leatino said, a warning clear in his tone. "You know your father doesn't like you to go there. He thinks it's too dangerous."

"Just a quick trip?" E'lofi gave the big male a pleading look. "I know you won't let anything happen to us. Please?"

Somehow Kate wasn't surprised when he sighed and agreed. As she had told Kate the night before, the girl was extremely good at getting what she wanted. But as Kate stared wide-eyed at the bustling market, she was glad Leatino had given in. The market reminded her of a cross between a middle eastern bazaar and a bar from a science fiction movie. It was the first place she had been where there were almost as many aliens as Mafanans.

The packed stalls were covered by brightly colored canopies and offered an astonishing variety of products for sale. Vendors yelled out their wares or bargained heatedly with their customers. E'lofi skipped along, choosing a tray of sweets here, a collection of glittering bracelets there, and a number of other small, colorful items. Her bodyguards stoically took charge of her purchases.

Kate trailed along behind her, content just to observe, until they passed a stall heaped with colorful scrolls. They reminded her of the scrolls so frequently piled on A'tai's desk, and she stopped to look.

"Very ancient," the vendor assured her, rushing to her side. He was a weathered Mafanan male. "And very rare."

"I'm sure." She suspected they were more likely mass

produced in this world's version of China, but they were beautifully done. A deep green scroll caught her eye, and she recognized the name Namoa in the intricate script.

As she debated purchasing it for A'tai, a small body barreled into her side and she looked down to see a young Mafanan boy. He gave her a wide grin as he apologized, then started to dart away.

A big hand clamped down on the boy's shoulder instead.

"Return it immediately," Leatino ordered.

"Return what?" she asked.

"He picked your pocket."

Sure enough, her small collection of coins had disappeared.

"I don't know what you're talking about," the boy whined, just as E'lofi came rushing over.

"What happened?" she asked, her eyes sparkling.

Leatino turned to tell her, and the boy took advantage of his momentary distraction to wiggle out from under his grip. He turned to run—and collided with A'tai.

A'tai snatched him up and tossed him back to Leatino, his outraged glare never leaving her face. His whole body was flushed red with anger. Oops.

"Home. Now," he ordered.

"See?" E'lofi whispered. "Intense."

"Umm, yeah. Thank you for the shopping trip. I hope we can—"

She didn't get a chance to finish the sentence before A'tai pulled her against his side and half-marched, half-carried her back towards the palace.

"Are your meetings finished?" she asked breathlessly.

"Yes." His face could have been etched from granite.

"Do you have any more?" she tried again.

"Yes. But they will wait until I've dealt with you."

That sounded disturbingly ominous, but her own temper was beginning to flare. "Why are you so angry?"

He came to a halt so quickly that she would have stumbled if he hadn't held her upright. "Do you really want to do this now? Here?"

They had reached the forecourt of the palace and they were surrounded by interested faces.

"I guess not."

"Good."

He resumed the forced march, and she bit her lip and did her best to keep up. As soon as the door to their quarters closed behind them, he whirled around to face her.

"Where in the Sisters were you?"

"You know where I was—you just found me there."

"After searching for you for over an hour. Why didn't you tell me where you were going?"

"You weren't here! You said you were going to be in meetings all day."

"That doesn't mean I didn't want to know where you were. I expected to find you where I left you!"

"I'm not some kind of toy you can put on a shelf until you're ready to play with me. First it was the lab, and now this."

"I built you a lab!"

"So you wouldn't have to let me out of your sight!"

They glared at each other, both of them panting. A door opened somewhere close by, letting in the sound of conversation, and he grabbed her hand and led her to the bedroom. His grip was gentle, despite his anger, but inescapable.

"Don't you know what could have happened to you?" he demanded, once they were in the bedroom. "The market is exactly the type of place where someone might try and abduct you."

Her heart skipped a beat. Was that true? Or was he just

being the same overly possessive male who had flipped out because she danced with another male? The colorful, bustling market had seemed safe enough.

"We had two bodyguards with us," she pointed out.

He snorted. "Some bodyguards. They let that boy rob you. Would they even have noticed if someone tried to steal you away from me?"

The fact that he might have a point only made her angrier. E'lofi's bodyguards had been much more focused on the girl than on her. She forced herself to take a deep breath.

"I promise you that I was perfectly safe. I know I should have left you a message, and next time—"

"There will not be a next time."

"What do you mean?"

"You are not going anywhere without me again."

"You're insane!"

"Then you are responsible for my insanity. I will keep you safe if I have to keep you locked in this room for the next ten years."

He turned and strode towards the door.

"A'tai, wait. Listen to me!"

"No," he said and left, slamming the door behind him with an ominous click.

When she tried to open the door, she discovered that it was locked. Her eyes narrowed as her anger escalated. He thought he could confine her to their bedroom? They'd just have to see about that.

A'TAI WAS STILL PACING ANGRILY WHEN HIS MOTHER appeared at the entrance to his study. Despite his rage, he had been wrestling with the urge to return and apologize to Kate—even though she was clearly in the wrong—and the last thing he needed was to listen to more of his mother's complaints. His first impulse was to demand that she leave, but since she so rarely made the effort to visit his quarters, it must be important.

"Do you need something, Mother?"

Instead of responding, she drifted into the room. She scanned the red still flickering on his skin, then moved away to casually examine the contents of his shelves. He prayed for patience.

"Where is your... mate?" she asked finally, fingering a colorful geode.

He started to tell her it was none of her business, then sighed. He suspected she already knew. "Confined to my quarters. She took a foolish risk, and I will not permit her to repeat that."

"Yes, I heard." U'rsul arranged herself gracefully in the chair by the window and studied his face. "You are so much like your father."

"Is that what you came to tell me?"

She ignored him, studying her manicured hands. "You know, I really did love your father very much. I suspect you don't believe me, but it's quite true."

He shrugged uncomfortably. "I believe you enjoyed having him care for you."

"You really don't understand." She gazed out the window. "I was thrilled when he chose me as his mate. He was so big and handsome and ambitious. I dreamed of us working together to strengthen the House."

He believed her. While he didn't remember her participating in House affairs while his father was alive, she had been invaluable since then.

"You were very helpful after he died," he admitted.

"And yet you never wondered why I knew so much?" Her gaze was unnervingly penetrating. "I was always interested, but

I discovered early in our union that was not what he wanted from me. He wanted a helpless female that he could care for and protect."

"I don't believe you." Or did he? He suddenly remembered a time when he was very young. His mother had taken him sailing, and they had been gone for most of the day. Despite a series of mishaps, they'd had a delightful day, but they had returned to find his father enraged. As enraged as he had been this morning.

"You don't have to believe me." His mother rose and adjusted her gown. "But consider this. What do you truly want? An intelligent female who will share your life? Or a possession that you can wrap in silk and only bring out to play with?"

Without giving him a chance to respond, she slipped out of the room.

"I'm not like that," he protested to the empty room. But there was an uncomfortable ring of truth to her words. With her quick intelligence and her surprising perspective on things, Kate was more than capable of being a true partner to him.

And yet since they had arrived in Kapenta, all he'd been able to think about was how many ways she could be hurt. Or taken from him.

By the Sisters, his mother was right. He needed to find his mate and apologize. But when he opened the locked door, their chamber was empty. Kate had vanished.

CHAPTER TWENTY-ONE

The lock gave a quiet click, and Kate smiled with satisfaction as the door swung open. Just as she had suspected back on the Ithyian ship, a piece of foil interrupted the electronic signal and released the lock. A small dish of sweets from her uneaten breakfast had provided the foil and it had taken only a few moments to open the lock. She knew that A'tai was driven by concern, but she'd be damned if she was going to let anybody lock her in a room.

She stepped out into the hallway, then hesitated. Now that she was free, what was she going to do? If her lab had been ready, she would have gone and done some work, but the equipment had not yet arrived. As she considered the possibilities, she remembered the scroll she had been examining before A'tai arrived on the scene and stormed off with her. Perfect.

She would make a quick trip to the market and purchase the scroll for him. It would show him that she could take care of herself, but hopefully the gift would also show him that she loved him in spite of his ridiculous overprotectiveness.

After a moment's thought, she returned to the room long

enough to retrieve a knife from the breakfast table. While she still thought he had been overreacting, it wouldn't hurt to be prepared. The knife was small but quite sharp, and it made her feel better to have it in her pocket.

Just as she reached the entrance foyer, Uauna appeared. The two of them stared at each other.

"May I assist you, Lady Kate?"

"I'm just going out for a little while," she said as casually as possible.

"Shall I call for an escort?"

For a moment, she was tempted to agree, but the purpose of this trip was to show A'tai she was capable of looking after herself. She shook her head. "I don't think that's necessary."

She suspected that Uauna wanted to object, but all he did was suggest tentatively, "Perhaps a cloak?"

Now that she would accept. There had been a wide variety of species at the market, but there was no reason to call attention to her appearance.

"Yes, please."

Uauna nodded and opened a hidden panel in the wall to reveal a selection of garments. He handed her a long green cloak. It covered her body, but it was made from a lightweight material that would not be oppressive in the heat of the day.

"Thank you, Uauna," she said sincerely.

"If you will permit me, Lady Kate, will you be gone long?"

"No. I'm just going to make a quick trip to the market."

He clearly wanted to object, but instead he reluctantly nodded.

"Yes, my lady." He hesitated. "You will be careful?"

"Of course."

As casually as she could, she walked past him and out the door. Would he immediately turn around and send A'tai after her? Determined to get a head start, she hurried through the palace and out into the streets. The guards stationed in the forecourt of the palace, were only interested in who was entering, not who was leaving, and paid little attention to her.

The market was easy enough to find, but even though it was still a fascinating spectacle of sights and smells and sounds, it felt a lot more ominous than it had before. People jostled against her, and she saw several males eyeing her appreciatively. She hadn't realized how much difference it had made to have the two large bodyguards behind her.

As quickly as possible, she made her way back to the bookseller's stall. The purchase didn't take long, and she suspected she had significantly overpaid, but she wasn't inclined to haggle. Breathing a sigh of relief, she turned to head back to the palace and ran into a thick, hairy body.

A familiar unpleasant smell hit her just as a hand clamped down on her arm.

"Gotcha."

Eshak had found her.

"Don't even think of making a sound," he snarled. "You're an escaped slave, and there are severe penalties for escaping your rightful owner."

She frantically tried to remember what A'tai had told her about the Imperial laws governing slavery. She had meant to look them up, but once he had told her that she was free, it had seemed less important than solving the riddle of the algae damage.

"You abandoned me here," she hissed, but she didn't quite dare to raise her voice. "A negligent slave owner isn't entitled to keep his slaves."

He laughed. "I don't intend to keep you. I'm going to sell you. But first, you're going to pay me back for all the trouble you've caused me."

To hell with that. She opened her mouth to scream, and his hand tightened with bone crushing force.

"If you ever want to know what happened to the other females, you will keep your mouth shut."

That threat stunned her into silence. She had to find out what he knew about Mary and Lily. Reaching into her pocket, she felt the reassuring handle of the knife. She wished it was bigger, but hopefully it would give her time to get away. The scroll was in the same pocket, and she suddenly had an idea. She had absolutely no doubt that A'tai would come looking for her, but she didn't know how long it would take him to find her.

Was the scroll distinctive enough that he would recognize the pieces? It was a long shot at best, but she started tearing off small sections and letting them flutter to the ground behind her as Eshak dragged her along.

One or two people frowned at the two of them, but no one made any attempt to stop him. He headed for the edge of the market, and her heart pounded even harder as he pulled her into a narrow alley. The sounds of the market immediately began to fade away behind them as she dropped the last few pieces of the scroll.

As soon as they were in the shadows of the alley, he shoved her up against the wall. He released her arm, only to seize her shoulder and start forcing her to the ground.

"On your knees, bitch."

His fingers dug painfully into her muscles, but she refused to give him the satisfaction of crying out as she obeyed. Her hand tightened on the knife as he unfastened his pants to reveal a short, hairy cock. He smelled even worse here, and her stomach threatened to rebel. As he grabbed her hair and started to drag her towards him, she whipped out the knife and pressed the tip into the base of his cock.

He froze.

"Let go of my hair," she ordered, and he snarled, but obeyed.

"Now tell me where my friends are."

"No. I don't think you have the guts to cut me," he taunted her, even though he didn't attempt to move.

Was he right? She could see a drop of purplish blood oozing from around the point of the knife, and her stomach rolled again.

"You're going to pay for this, human," he warned. "I was only going to play with you a little, but you just made things a whole lot worse."

Despite the threat, he still hadn't moved, but then again, neither had she, and she realized that they were at a standstill. In order to get away from him, she would have to lift the knife, and she suspected that as soon as she did, he would go for it. Her chances of keeping it away from him were slim at best. She didn't think she had the stomach to seriously injure him, and she tried desperately to think of an alternative. Her arm was already getting tired.

He smirked down at her and she suspected he was getting ready to try and seize the knife. His legs tensed, but before he could move, a big body came out of nowhere and smashed him into the wall.

A'tai had found her.

A'TAI CURLED HIS LIMB AROUND THE SLAVER'S NECK UNTIL his eyes bulged. He was shaking from fear as much as anger. He had come so close to losing Kate.

He had still been staring in disbelief at the empty bedroom when Uauna had found him.

"I've been looking for you, sire. Did you know that Lady Kate was returning to the market? Alone?"

His eyes closed for a second in horrified despair before he turned and raced down the stairs, Uauna following close behind. He had been an idiot to try and confine her.

"You didn't try and stop her?" he snapped.

"I am not a jailer," Uauna said reproachfully.

The other male was right, and he would have to apologize to him later, but right now finding Kate was the only thing that mattered.

"She is wearing a green cloak," Uauna called after him as he charged out the door.

Not sure where else to go, he headed for the stall where he had found her earlier. His chest ached when the vendor described her purchase, and he realized that she had bought it for him. But then the male told him that after buying the scroll, she had been escorted away by an Ithyian male. His blood ran cold. Even if it wasn't her original captor, the Ithyians were notorious slavers.

He frantically scanned the market, looking for any trace of a green cloak. He thought he caught a glimpse of green and started after it, only to collide with an elderly female. As he steadied her, he saw a piece of green paper fluttering at her feet. He automatically noted it as part of a Namoan scroll, then froze. Could it be a piece of the one Kate had purchased?

His heart pounding, he started searching for other scraps. They had been scattered by the constant activity, but enough remained to lead him towards the edge of the market. He almost missed the last one at the entrance to the alley, but then he saw a flash of green and saw the Ithyian leaning over Kate.

Now this bastard was going to die.

"Wait," Kate said, clutching his arm. "Don't kill him."

"You wish to save his life?"

"Not at all. But he said he knew what happened to my friends."

"Wouldn't you like to know?" the Ithyian sneered as A'tai reluctantly loosened his grip.

"Yes, I would." He slammed him up against the wall again. "And if you wish to live, you'll tell me."

The male gave him a sullen look, but when A'tai tightened his grip again, he finally muttered, "I don't know. The trackers seem to be defective. The captain sent one of us to each of the planets in the system. Waste of fucking time. But this one just walked right into me. Stupid female."

He automatically slammed the male against the wall again at the insult, but he was more concerned about the fact that Kate's face had paled.

"Other planets?" she whispered.

"Are you all right, amali?" He wanted to pull her into his arms, but he couldn't let go of the Ithyian. He settled for curling a limb around her back.

"They could be anywhere." A tear slid down her cheek, and his heart ached for her.

"There are only two other planets in this system. We will find them."

"Only two?" she asked with a despairing laugh.

"Yeah, good luck with that," the Ithyian sneered.

A'tai growled and tightened his limb around the male's neck until his body went limp. He had no further use for the bastard.

"Is he dead?" Kate asked, but she didn't seem particularly concerned.

"No." He let the male's body fall to the ground, then wrapped his arms around her. "Unfortunately. But I will pass him over to the Imperial Guard. He will spend the rest of his life on one of the prison planets—and he will undoubtedly wish that I had killed him." She pressed closer to him as he continued. "But he no longer concerns you. We at least know that your friends are in this system and not prisoners of the Ithyians."

"I just feel so helpless. Three planets to search."

"We are already searching here on Mafana—and I will have my mother spread the word as well."

"That should thrill her," she said dryly.

"You might be surprised. She told me I was not treating you appropriately. And she was right. I was coming to apologize when I found you missing." He bent his head, his forehead touching hers. "I was terrified that I would lose you forever."

"I was going to come back. I don't want to lose you either." She sighed. "You were right about the market, but you can't treat me like a child. I thought you were overreacting again."

"I wasn't, but I can see why you would believe that. I know you are a strong, intelligent female—but you are also fragile. My instincts will always demand that I protect you."

She started to speak, but he put a gentle finger across her lips. "I promise that I will do my best to restrain that instinct as much as possible."

"Good. Because I would hate to have to keep escaping."

He growled and kissed her. She melted happily into his embrace. By the time he lifted his head, his skin was edged with gold and he caught the sweet scent of her arousal.

"Does the idea of chasing me down excite you?" she teased.

"Perhaps. Does the idea of being caught excite you?"

He unfurled two of his limbs and gripped her arms. The delightful pink washed over her face, but she shook her head.

"We can talk about that later. When we're alone," she added as the Ithyian groaned. "Tell me about these other two planets."

"Sayari is mainly a nature preserve for affluent Tajiri families. They have vacation homes and hunting lodges there, along with a few resorts for wealthy guests from other systems."

"Hunting? They wouldn't hunt a female, would they?"

"Of course not," he said soothingly, hoping he was correct. "I will ask that we be notified if a human is discovered, although the Tajiri are fickle creatures."

"Why? What are they like?"

"Rich, arrogant bastards." His mouth curled in distaste.

"Are they princes?" she asked innocently.

One of his arms tapped her bottom, and she jumped, the scent of her arousal increasing.

"No, my amali," he growled. "They simply have too many credits for their own good. Yangu is their home planet, and the only other habitable planet in our system. It will be the most difficult to search. Because of its natural stores of gemstones, it is very rich and attracts a lot of traffic—not always of the most desirable type. I think it might be best to offer a reward there as well."

"Can you afford that?"

"I'm a rich, arrogant bastard, remember? And yes, *we* can afford it."

She smiled up at him.

"But first, I need to take this bastard to the guard. I will send for an escort—" He came to an abrupt halt, and forced himself to ask. "Will you accept an escort back to the palace?"

"Of course I will—but thank you for asking."

CHAPTER TWENTY-TWO

Kate curled up in the window seat in their bedroom and stared thoughtfully out across the sea. A'tai had—very reluctantly—left her for another one of his seemingly endless meetings. It had been two days since Eshak had tried to take her and she still wasn't sleeping or eating well. The feel of his hand dragging her away haunted her.

A soft knock sounded on the door, immediately followed by E'lofi peeping into the room, her eyes sparkling.

"Hi. Would you like a visitor?"

"Please. I'm tired of my own thoughts."

The girl walked in with her graceful, dancing step. She really was extremely pretty and it was hard to believe sometimes that A'tai had chosen her instead.

"You look like you have some interesting gossip," she teased.

E'lofi laughed. "Did you hear? Mafana has banned Ithyian ships. Forever."

"Really?" An unexpected feeling of relief swept over her. Maybe she could stop having nightmares now.

"Yes. A'tai made a very impassioned speech and I made sure my father supported him."

"That was sweet. Thank you."

The girl shrugged. "I'm not sure if it was necessary—no one really likes them anyway—but I thought it couldn't hurt."

"Can you stay for a little while? I'll ring for some tea."

"Of course. I have to tell you all about my new gowns."

But when Uauna brought the tray, it contained three cups. She gave him a puzzled frown, but before he could say anything, the door opened again and U'rsul swept in. The room seemed to shrink, but she managed to smile.

"Welcome, Lady U'rsul. Are you joining us for tea?"

"Yes. I brought some of my special blend in case you were low on supplies."

Kate gritted her teeth. "Uauna makes sure that we are well-stocked."

"Really? It's usually a job for the lady of the house. But then again, you have your own... interests."

Would A'tai object if she threw his mother out of the window, she wondered, as E'lofi stepped into the breach.

"Is that the parjan leaves, Lady U'rsul? My aunt always spoke most highly of it. She said it was the only thing she could tolerate when she was bearing her first child."

U'rsul gave her a gracious smile. "That's correct. I'm afraid not everyone appreciates it."

Patience, Kate told herself.

"Shall I pour?" E'lofi stepped into the silence again.

"Please," Kate said.

E'lofi performed the small ritual as gracefully as she did everything and Kate saw U'rsul watching her wistfully. When the girl handed her a cup, Kate took it reluctantly. She found most Mafanan teas very bitter, and she suspected U'rsul would be scandalized if Kate dumped a pound of sweetener into her cup. She took a cautious sip, but to her relief it only had a slight lemony taste that was unexpectedly refreshing.

"This is delicious," she said sincerely, and U'rsul inclined her head graciously.

Kate sipped her tea in silence as the other two females discussed current affairs. She recognized some of the names—E'lofi had been teaching her—but she was content to stay out of the conversation.

"Oh my, look at the time." E'lofi suddenly jumped up. She shot Kate an apologetic look. "I was supposed to meet Lady R'ian half an hour ago, and I don't want her to think I'm late."

Kate laughed. "Then you'd better run."

E'lofi bent down and kissed her cheek. "I'll be back tomorrow."

Then she vanished through the door, leaving Kate alone with U'rsul.

"Such a delightful girl," U'rsul said wistfully.

"Yes, she is. I'm very fond of her."

"She seems to enjoy your company as well." There was the slightest hint of surprise in U'rsul's voice.

"I'm nice to the people I like."

To her surprise, U'rsul laughed. "Now why do I feel as if I am not included in that category?"

"Because you've made it quite clear that you disapprove of the fact that I am A'tai's mate," she said bluntly. She was tired and her stomach hurt and she didn't want to play games.

"Actually, I have reconsidered."

Kate almost dropped her teacup. "What?"

"My son assumed responsibility of our House when his father died, even though he was far too young. He worked very hard and he has been very successful—but he has never really enjoyed it. It did not make him happy." Cold golden eyes surveyed her. "You, I think, make him happy."

She had the oddest urge to cry. "We make each other happy."

"That is how it should be." U'rsul rose gracefully to her feet. "You are looking very pale, even for a human. Tell A'tai to take you back to Ataian."

"Really?" Her heart skipped a beat as she thought wistfully of their peaceful life on the island.

U'rsul shrugged a shoulder. "There are no pressing business matters that I cannot handle, and since neither of you appear to enjoy the social season, there's no real reason for you to remain. I might ask E'lofi to come and stay for a while. She has immense potential."

"I agree."

Golden eyes swept over her again. "I will send more of the parjan tea to accompany you."

"Thank you."

"Tell A'tai to see me before you leave."

U'rsul departed in a swirl of perfumed skirts, and Kate breathed a sigh of relief. That had gone better than she expected, but she still found A'tai's mother overwhelming.

She drank the rest of the tea, watching the birds circling over the water. Her eyes felt heavy, and her stomach had calmed for the first time in days. It must have been because of E'lofi's news, she decided as she poured herself another cup of tea, smiling as she remembered the conversation.

She continued to replay the discussion as she curled back up in the window seat, then froze.

The only thing her aunt could tolerate...

It couldn't be possible, could it?

. . .

When A'tai entered their bedroom, he found Kate sitting immobile on the window seat.

"Good afternoon, my amali. I heard my mother came to visit. Are you all right?"

She looked up at him, her pale skin even paler than usual. What had his mother done now?

"Do you know a doctor?" she whispered.

Fear raced through him so quickly his limbs almost buckled. He knew she hadn't been eating or sleeping well, but he had blamed it on the incident in the market. What if something more serious was wrong? He tried to think as he reached down to pick her up. Fuck, she even felt lighter in his arms.

"I'll take you there right now."

"No! Wait. Can he come here?"

"It will be faster if I take you."

"No." She started to struggle as he reached the door. "Listen to me."

His body screamed for action but he forced himself to pause. "What is it, my Kate?"

"Can't he come here instead?"

"But—"

"Please."

He had promised to listen to her, he reminded himself. "If that is what you wish."

As he reached for the communicator, she stopped him again. "Is he discreet? He won't tell anyone?"

He'd never been a huge fan of Physician Hollia because of the way he pandered to his mother, but he had never known the male to reveal any confidential information. "He is very discreet."

"Then please send for him."

As soon as he completed the call, he tried to carry her to the bed, but she insisted that he take her back to the window seat instead.

"Will you please tell me what's wrong, amali?"

"I don't think anything is wrong—but I want to be sure."

Her lips curved in an odd little smile, and for some reason, he relaxed a little. The fact that she was curled so snugly in his arms, her body warm against his, also helped to sooth him.

"And nothing happened with my mother?"

"She told me I make you happy."

"And she is right." His own lips twisted. "Not something I say very often."

"I told her you make me happy as well."

He couldn't resist, bending his head to kiss her. He was still tasting her lips when the door chime sounded, then the physician rushed in.

"What's wrong? I understand Lady Kate is ill?"

"Tell him what's wrong, amali," he urged.

"A'tai, I know this is going to be difficult, but please trust me. Can you leave us alone?"

Leave her alone? With a strange male? When her health could be in danger? He wanted to roar his refusal, but she only waited, watching him patiently, her eyes warm with understanding.

"I will be outside the door," he growled, reluctance in every line of his body as he left the room.

He immediately regretted the decision, his hand going to open the door multiple times, but each time he forced himself to wait. Fortunately for the sake of his sanity, he did not have long to wait before Physician Hollia emerged beaming.

"Is she ill?" he demanded.

"Not at all. Go and see for yourself."

He wanted to wring some answers out of the male, but his

mate was more important. He rushed into the room, finding her still on the window seat, her head bowed.

"Kate?"

She looked up at him, tears streaming down her cheeks. He was going to kill the fucking physician, he decided coldly, even as he kneeled in front of her. He'd had the nerve to smile at him after leaving his mate in tears?

"Whatever it is, it's fine. We'll fight it. I'll arrange for a flight to—"

"A'tai, stop. Everything's fine. There's nothing to fight." She took his hand and placed it on her stomach. "We're going to have a baby."

What? He could hear the sound of the sea ringing in his ears as his limbs collapsed.

"A'tai! A'tai! Do I need to get the doctor back?" Kate bent over him, her face worried.

"A baby?" he whispered. "Did you say we're having a baby?"

"Yes. Isn't it wonderful?"

"But you said it wasn't possible."

She grinned at him. "I didn't think it was, but I was wrong. Aren't you happy?"

"Happy?" The word sounded much too tame, too inadequate to express his feelings. "I have never been happier."

He pulled her close, kissing her until they were both breathless, his limbs wrapped carefully around her stomach. A stomach that sheltered a new life.

He suddenly realized there was so much to be done.

"We have to prepare," he told her. "I'll arrange for a nurse, or perhaps two. Perhaps it would be better to have the physician move in as well. We'll need a nursery—"

Kate put a finger across his lips. "Yes, we will need a nursery, but not here. It's time we went home, back to Ataian."

The thought delighted him, but he hesitated. "I will need to let my mother know. Both that we are leaving and about the child."

"I think she already suspects about the baby," she said thoughtfully. "Maybe that's why she was so... pleasant. And she was the one who said we should go."

A huge wave of relief washed over him.

"Thank the Sisters. Let's go home."

EPILOGUE

A'tai paced back and forth, scowling at Osaga, their midwife.

"Are you sure this birthing pool is large enough? I'm sure the one in the palace was twice this size."

Osaga didn't bother to answer him, rolling her eyes at Kate. She smiled at the other female, then put her hand on her back and gave a soft sigh. A'tai immediately stopped pacing and rushed over to her.

"Are you all right? Is it time?"

"Not yet," she assured him. "I was simply thinking that I'm glad the pool isn't any larger. You know I can't breathe underwater, and I might slip in a bigger pool."

"I will be supporting you the entire time." His brows drew together. "But if you would be more comfortable with a smaller one, perhaps I could have another one built—"

"That would be too small," she said firmly, ignoring Osaga's snort. "This one is just right."

"But—"

"I think the midday heat is increasing. Why don't you take me back to our chamber so I can rest?"

"Of course, my amali."

He promptly lifted her into his arms, the huge mound of her stomach not the slightest deterrent, and headed for the door.

"I can walk, you know."

"But I prefer to carry you." He smiled down at her. "I cannot wait until I can carry both you and our daughter."

"Or son."

He shrugged. "I believe it is a daughter."

His expression was as arrogant as ever, but she could see the love in his eyes. Her heart gave that little skip it always did when he looked at her like that. She raised her hand and stroked along the sensitive edge of his gills.

"Since you aren't going to let me get any exercise by walking, maybe we could find some other method?"

Hunger washed over his face, golden eyes gleaming.

"What did you have in mind?"

"Maybe a little... riding would be good for me?" she asked innocently.

He jolted, and then his pace sped up until he was almost running. Gold flickered across his skin.

As he carried her into the tower room she had chosen for their bedroom, she couldn't help looking around with a smile. All of the windows in the ancient stone walls were open, the long white curtains fluttering in the gentle sea breeze. After an extended discussion they had agreed that the castle on Ataian was a more suitable option than the farmhouse.

Since they had decided not to return to Kapenta on a permanent basis, the castle provided more options for entertaining and the constant House business. U'rsul continued to manage the House affairs in the city, but their relationship remained... complicated.

The fact that she was a four-hour boat ride away, rather than a four-minute walk, had helped, since U'rsul's brief softness had not lasted long. But Kate couldn't deny that she relieved A'tai from the social functions he so disliked, and she seemed genuinely excited about the upcoming birth.

"Why are you smiling?" he asked as he laid her in the center of the big, round bed.

"I'm just glad we're alone." She caught the flash of guilt that washed across his face. "What?"

"About that..."

"A'tai," she said warningly.

"My mother will be here to attend the birth," he admitted. "It would be a great insult if she did not come."

"I wouldn't be insulted," she muttered, then sighed. "But I suppose it's only fair that she meet her grandson."

"Or granddaughter," he said firmly. "And she is bringing E'lofi with her."

"That part will be nice anyway." The girl had been to visit several times and Kate always enjoyed her company.

A'tai hesitated again. "Mother also told me she might have some news about your friends."

"Really?" She tried to struggle upright, but gravity and her stomach were against her. "What did she say?"

"Exactly what I told you. You know how she is."

"Infuriating?" She gave up the struggle and laid back against the pillows. As excited as she was by the possibility that U'rsul might actually have news about Mary and Lily, she wasn't going to pin her hopes on it. "I just hope our son—"

"Or daughter."

"—doesn't take after her."

"Why should she? I'm nothing like my mother."

Since he made the statement with the exact look of supercilious distaste that so frequently crossed U'rsul's face, she couldn't help laughing. For a moment he looked even more offended, but then he relaxed and smiled at her.

"You certainly know how to deflate my ego, my Kate."

"Your ego can stand it." She ran a teasing hand down his chest and between his limbs, her fingers skating along the edge of his sheath. "I just hope nothing else is deflated."

"My moa is always anxious for you."

That was certainly true, even when she felt as awkward and ungainly as she did now. She tried to sit up again, then huffed with frustration. "You'll have to help me."

"Of course."

In a matter of seconds he had her poised over his stomach, two of his limbs supporting her back as two others slid her gown over her shoulders. They gently circled her sensitive breasts. He had been fascinated with her breasts before, but he had been awed by the way they had grown with her pregnancy. His gentle suction had already drawn drops of milk from her swollen nipples, and a few drops beaded there now. His eyes darkened, and she felt his moa stir beneath her.

"Definitely not deflated," she murmured, as he parted her legs, a velvety sucker teasing her clit.

"Come for me, amali." He thrust into her pussy as his suckers clamped down on her nipples and clit at the same time.

Her body obeyed, rocking helplessly into a shuddering climax.

"That wasn't fair," she said, when her breathing finally slowed.

"No?" Golden eyes laughed up at her, warm with love and desire.

"I'm supposed to be riding you."

His limbs undulated beneath her, rocking her gently back and forth.

"And you are. But I want to see how many times I can make you come before I can no longer resist this sweet little cunt."

"Okay," she whispered breathlessly as he caught hold of her arms.

Five times, as it turned out.

She sprawled against his side, limp with satisfaction, as he gently stroked her stomach.

"Are you happy, my Kate?" he asked.

"Perfectly, exquisitely happy."

"Do you miss your old life?"

"Not at all. I still have my work. But more importantly, I have you. And soon we'll have our son."

"Our daughter."

She shook her head. "You're so persistent. We should place a bet on whether it's a boy or a girl."

"Why? Either way will be a win."

And when, a month later, their daughter was placed in her arms, her pale skin still wet from the birthing pool, and looked up at her with big golden eyes, she knew that he was right.

She glanced up to find U'rsul smiling at her from across the room, her own golden eyes wet with tears. E'lofi was crying as well. Having the two of them attend the birth had not been as bad as she feared. Both of them had been supportive during her labor. E'lofi had been her usual cheerful self, somehow managing to make Kate laugh despite the pressure building in her body. U'rsul, of course, was far more restrained, but she had succeeded in calming A'tai when he started to panic as Kate's labor grew more intense. Nonetheless, she was glad he had refused to allow U'rsul to fill the room with spectators in the traditional manner.

A'tai's cheek was pressed against her as he looked down at the baby. He was completely wrapped around her, his arms supporting her upper body as his limbs had supported her lower body during the birth. His finger gently caressed the baby's cheek, and she immediately opened her mouth and tried to suckle on it.

"She is hungry, amali." He sounded almost panicked, and she found herself smiling. He was going to be a wonderful, but insanely protective, father.

She gently helped the baby find her nipple, then cradled her close. The baby had already assumed her land form, her legs curled into a close semblance to chubby little human legs. But then one limb unfurled, reaching up to pat her breast, and she laughed.

"Like father, like daughter," she murmured.

"Her father will be most happy to show you the difference," he whispered in her ear, his cool breath sending a shiver down her spine despite her exhaustion.

"Don't even think about it, Prince A'tai," Osaga said firmly as she handed Kate a silky cloth to wrap around the baby, and Kate felt herself blush. "You must wait at least a month."

Blue flickered across A'tai's skin as well, but he frowned at the midwife. "I would never damage my mate."

"Of course, you wouldn't," E'lofi said soothingly as she and U'rsul came to admire the baby. "She's very beautiful, Kate. What are you going to name her?"

"I thought perhaps, Marli."

"For your friends." A'tai understood immediately, his arms

tightening around her. "I am sure they will be delighted once we find them."

Her heart ached for her missing friends, but she did her best to be optimistic that they would eventually succeed in finding the other women. U'rsul had actually uncovered a rumor about a strange, redheaded female involved with the heir to one of the wealthy Tajiri merchant families, but the details were annoyingly vague. The male in question sounded like a wealthy playboy, and Kate could only hope that if Lily was with him she was being treated well. The couple were supposedly sequestered on Sayari, and A'tai was trying to use his connections to gather more information from the elite planet.

There had been no word about Mary, but A'tai's agents continued to search.

"Her name will be M'rli," U'rsul announced, interrupting Kate's thoughts. "She is heir to the House of Maulimu."

Kate fought back a sigh. As much as she'd dreaded U'rsul's arrival, A'tai's mother had proven unexpectedly comforting. She had been determined that nothing would disturb the last days of Kate's pregnancy, and her complete conviction that the birth would go smoothly had buoyed Kate's confidence. However, it now appeared that she was reverting to her old self.

"I'm really quite exhausted," U'rsul continued, her voice faint.

"You weren't the one giving birth, Mother," A'tai snapped.

"Why don't we go and have some tea?" E'lofi suggested smoothly, putting her arm in U'rsul's and guiding her out of the room. She looked back over her shoulder at Kate and winked.

"That girl is going to have this whole planet at her feet," Kate laughed. "I think you missed out on something special there, A'tai."

"I found something far more special." His eyes glowed as he

looked down at her and M'rli. "A beautiful female from a primitive planet."

"And I found an alien octopus man." He frowned as he always did when she called him that, and she stroked a teasing hand down his chest. "And the only male I have ever wanted. Do you think we can wait a whole month?"

Gold flickered across his skin. "I'm quite sure I can find ways to pleasure you before then, but I will wait as long as necessary. We have all the time in the world."

Even Osaga had left, and now it was just the three of them in the quiet room, the sea murmuring gently outside the open windows. M'rli's eyes were closed, her small lips still pursed. Kate tucked her closer, then smiled and closed her eyes, knowing that A'tai would watch over them.

He was right. They had all the time they needed. Time to find her friends and time to raise their daughter. Time to work and time to study. But most of all, time to love.

AUTHOR'S NOTE

Thank you so much for reading **Kate and the Kraken**!

I really enjoyed being back in the Alien Abduction universe. I had the idea for this story a long time ago, and I've been dying to get to the letter K! A'tai is a little more… alien than some of my heroes but I think that he and Kate are a perfect match!

Whether you enjoyed the story or not, it would mean the world to me if you left an honest review on Amazon – reviews are one of the best ways to help other readers find my books!

As always, I have to thank my readers for joining me on these adventures! Your support and encouragement make it possible for me to keep writing these books.

And, of course, a special thanks to my beta team – Janet S, Nancy V, and Kitty S. Your thoughts and comments are incredibly helpful!

AUTHOR'S NOTE

Lily's story is next and you know she's going to give her hero a run for his money - literally! Coming up in - ***Lily and the Lion***!

A wealthy, bored alien. A fierce, unlucky woman. A primitive hunting planet. Let the games begin!

Lily and the Lion is available on Amazon!

To make sure you don't miss out on any new releases, please visit my website and sign up for my newsletter!

www.honeyphillips.com

OTHER TITLES

The Alien Abduction Series

Anna and the Alien
Beth and the Barbarian
Cam and the Conqueror
Deb and the Demon
Ella and the Emperor
Faith and the Fighter
Greta and the Gargoyle
Hanna and the Hitman
Izzie and the Icebeast
Joan and the Juggernaut
Kate and the Kraken
Lily and the Lion

The Alien Invasion Series

Alien Selection
Alien Conquest
Alien Prisoner
Alien Breeder
Alien Alliance
Alien Hope

Exposed to the Elements
The Naked Alien
The Bare Essentials
A Nude Attitude
The Buff Beast
The Strip Down

Cyborgs on Mars
High Plains Cyborg
The Good, the Bad, and the Cyborg
A Fistful of Cyborg
A Few Cyborgs More
The Magnificent Cyborg
The Outlaw Cyborg

Treasured by the Alien
with Bex McLynn
Mama and the Alien Warrior
A Son for the Alien Warrior
Daughter of the Alien Warrior
A Family for the Alien Warrior
The Nanny and the Alien Warrior

Standalone Books
Jackie and the Giant - A Cosmic Fairy Tale
Krampus and the Crone - An SFR Holiday Tale

Anthologies

Alien Embrace

Pets in Space 6

ABOUT THE AUTHOR

Honey Phillips writes steamy science fiction stories about hot alien warriors and the human women they can't resist. From abductions to invasions, the ride might be rough, but the end always satisfies.

Honey wrote and illustrated her first book at the tender age of five. Her writing has improved since then. Her drawing skills, unfortunately, have not. She loves writing, reading, traveling, cooking, and drinking champagne - not necessarily in that order.

Honey loves to hear from her wonderful readers! You can stalk her on her website at
www.honeyphillips.com

Or at any of the following locations…

- amazon.com/author/honeyphillips
- facebook.com/honeyphillipsauthor
- instagram.com/honeyphillipsauthor
- bookbub.com/authors/honey-phillips

Printed in Dunstable, United Kingdom